Fairytales Poems & Prophecies

Mark J.T. Griffin

First Printed in 2009 in Great Britain

Cover Design
Mark J.T. Griffin

Published by

Power of One Ltd
Gryffyn House
Wyre Lane
Long Marston
Stratford upon Avon
CV37 8RQ

ISBN 0-9533017-3-7 (First Edition)

Contents

Acknowledgements

This book could not have been written without the help, encouragement and support of many and there are many without whom ideas could not have been transformed into print. I would therefore like to acknowledge the following for their motivation, stimulation, inspiration, guidance, help or contribution to the development of this book:

Ingrid for her love, patience and encouragement

and

My daughters, Dantje and Steph for their love

The Griffin and Grupping Families for support
Michael Moorcock and Douglas Adams for their words
Ridley Scott and Luc Besson for their images
Robin Williams and Billy Connolly for their humour
Jack Black and Mindstore for the spark
Rush, Marillion, Jon Anderson and Yes for their music
Ann Roodt, Bill and Gaynor Marshall for their friendship

Sam and Lily for interrupting. A lot.

Bramble who, like all cats,
seems to know something, but still isn't saying.

In Memory of Piers and David

And to the Visionaries, Poets and Perfects. Be the Light!

Author's Note

I began writing articles then later poems and short stories back in my early twenties as an escape from the logical/rational job, a computer programmer, which kept me in house, food and warmth. It wasn't a bad job - I really enjoyed it and there was something creative about solving problems. Creative writing, indeed any writing I approached, set different obstacles to overcome.

I started with a few "war stories" for various magazines and went on to writing short stories, which in many ways had the flavour of a Grimm's fairytale with the emphasis on "grim".

As I developed ideas some took on lives of their own and a few morphed into the novels that I have since published. Some are of course still under development, kept up my sleeve as future projects.

My influences are three-fold. Firstly songs – a few of the stories contained herein were based on lyrics which I felt were cinematic and could be freed from the bounds the song to become a full-blown short story. Secondly, I have been heavily influenced by '70s comedy writing – the greats, like Monty Python, Spike Milligan and Douglas Adams and I'm sure you'll taste their flavours within.

Finally, I have been influenced by my "New Age" beliefs, which have driven me for over thirty years. They amount to the simple belief of life everlasting and universal goodness. Again, this is a theme that runs through this collection.

This collection therefore amounts to over 25 years work. I was once told I could not write by one and should not write by another. I'm glad I ignored them. Once again, many thanks to my friends, family and the many others for their inspiration and turning a few passing dreams into a reality; it would not have been possible without you.

May You Make Your Dreams Last Longer Than The Night.....

December 2009

Once Upon a Time...

When you gaze into the night sky you can see
billions upon billions of stars.

More than there are grains of sand
on all the beaches on earth.

Their light shines on us from thousands of millions of years ago
from different times and from wonderful worlds.

Now rest your weary eyes my child.

Let the blankets warm and comfort you.

For I will tell you a story!

A story with dragons and witches and wizards.

With heroes and heroines from far-off lands
with strange-sounding names.

Stories of love and life and lost dreams.

For I am your storyteller

and

I have seen such wonders!

The Rain Maker

"Some say one's word is one's bond.
When words are broken, let the heavens fall."

For forty days and forty nights the plains had seen no rain. Not a drop. The rivers were dry and the wells were dust. The sun that beat down cooked the fields until they cracked like porcelain and had turned them to dirt.

It was about this time that the Rain Maker came into One Horse town. He carried a commodious battered burgundy carpetbag with a brass clasp and leather handles. His black hair was long, unkempt and was swept behinds his ears. It was held down with a black velvet broad-brimmed hat from which trailed a single crow's feather. His chiselled face was tanned a light brown and his dark eyes were keen and eagle-sharp. His face was Lakota Sioux. He wore a black suit; a white bleached calico shirt and a small dream catcher around his neck. He was protected from the plain's wind by a long black coat that swept the dust around his dark leather boots and rustled about him like a restless autumn breeze.

He walked down the dusty dry street and perhaps would have been ignored if it had not have been for his declaration. He dropped his bag in the dirt and raised his long hands to the cloudless blue sky and confidently spoke to whoever cared to listen.

"I can bring you the rain! I can bring you rain to grow your withering crops! I can bring you rain enough to fill your wells! I can bring you rain that will make life return to the farms and the fields. I can bring you the rain!"

Furrow-browed farmers looked up as they nursed empty beer glasses in the saloon. Worried worn women gossiping in the general store turned and walked to the window to see who made such a rash promise. Hungry toyless children stopped their play on the boardwalks. The wind whistled around the rooftops and blew coils of dust down Main Street and high into the sky.

The man smiled wryly. He knew they needed him and he knew they would ask. Then old Jethro Thomas, boldest and greediest of the farmers, walked into the street and broke the silence of the town with a sneer. "Stranger! Many have made the same promise! All have failed! Why are you any different?"

The man thought for a moment and turned to face the farmer, "There are many who claim to have the power but do not possess it. There are many who are bound to fail. But I cannot fail. I have faith! I have the gift! I will not break my word! I am the Rain Maker!" and with this affirmation he picked up his carpetbag and walked to the hotel.

At the desk he counted three coins from his deep coat pocket and placed them on the worn oak counter. "The room at the front is empty. It has a bath. I will have it. Tell your mayor he has a single day to make up his mind. Then I will be gone."

He turned and walked up the stairs to his room, opened the door and collapsed on the soft bed to rest after his long journey. Soon, though the sun beat through the window creating shadows of the lace curtains that danced on the opposite wall, he drifted into a light slumber.

An hour later there was a gentle knock at the door. Rising from the bed the Rain Maker opened it. It was the hotel manager. "Sir, some of the folks want to talk with you. I think they do want to hire you."

As he suspected, there was a deputation lead by the mayor of the dwindling population. "Can you really do it? We are a poor town you know? What is your price? What is you guarantee?"

The Rain Maker ran his thin fingers through his mane of dark hair and looked down to his dusty worn boots. Then, as he looked up he noticed the gold watch chain on the mayor's waistcoat, the diamond collar stud on the hotel owner's shirt and the guns at the sides of each of the farmers.

"My price is one hundred dollars." The farmers gasped with a sharp intake of breath but the rainmaker continued, "And my guarantee is simple. If it does not rain you do not pay me. I will keep my word," he said matter of factly.

The mayor seemed to confer with a couple of the farmers and then eagerly said "We will agree to your terms," but the Rain Maker noted the eagerness in the mayor's voice and a hint of betrayal which he had noted only once before.

And the Rain Maker said, "I trust you will not break you word."

The Rain Maker picked up his hat, long coat and carpetbag, walked down the stairs, through the bar and stepped from the hotel into Main Street. The townsfolk followed him, whispering behind his back and filed from the hotel and lined each side of the street expectantly. As the citizens waited, arms folded, the Rain Maker placed the bag in the centre of the street and knelt in the dust to unpack it.

He took out a black book, which he laid next to the bag. He next took from the bag a long tube. He took a glass jar of black powder and one of yellow powder and filled the tube with a mixture of each sealing the top of the tube with a cork. He then tied a short sharpened stick to the base with hemp creating a rocket. He stabbed the rocket into the ground and twisted a small piece of dry cord into the cork for a fuse.

Rising to his feet he spread his arms wide and raised his head to the cloudless blue sky. He chanted to the elements for respite. He chanted to the rain gods. He chanted to his ancestors to give him strength. And singing to the earth he whirled like a windmill and his coat spread out around him. He danced around the rocket, which quivered in the dirt, and he stomped in the dust as he sang his credo.

Then, abruptly, he stopped. He took out a box of matches from his pocket and reached down to the fuse, which he lit. His eyes were wild and staring and he took a few paces back from the sizzling rocket. Then he dropped to his knees clutching the book between his hands.

Suddenly with a loud *whoosh* the rocket flew skyward and was swallowed by the cloudless blue sky. Seconds later there was a distant explosion above him and the townsfolk gazed at each other in amazement.

What was this hocus pocus that they were being subjected to? Was this witchcraft, black magic or some sort of Indian medicine? When did this heathen ever go to church on a Sunday?

In the centre of Main Street the Rain Maker was kneeling in the dust, his head bowed and eyes tightly shut, clasping his hands around the book in prayer. His hands trembled and began to turn white as he wished and dreamed and visioned his prayers to be answered.

Within moments the sky above him began to darken. From out of the electric bright blue of the heavens, seemingly from nowhere wispy cotton clouds began to appear. And the small cotton buds of clouds grew in size and swirled about the sky as if orchestrated by a celestial conductor. Then the sky was full of heavy grey clouds that darkened to a sullen lead colour, heavy with rain. But still the Rain Maker prayed.

The first drop fell on the hat of the Rain Maker, dribbled onto his long coat and into the dust to disappear into the dirt. The next dribbled down the nose of the mayor, the next trickled down the forehead of Jethro Thomas, the next blossomed to the sleeve of his neighbour, the next on the head of a child, the next onto the forehead of a hound who took shelter under the boardwalk.

Then the drops turned to a drizzle. Then to a shower. Then to a downpour. Then into a deluge which rushed eagerly down the roofs and gullies into the gutters and then into the streets turning them into fast flowing rivers. It rained. Just as the Rain Maker had promised it would.

The townsfolk were now in the street, dancing in the puddles that formed in front of the store and the saloon and the hotel. They danced as if they were reborn. As if they had never seen rain before.

Above the dancing, lightening illuminated the buildings in a ghostly white, electric blue and thunder rolled and growled like an angry God.

A lightening bolt struck the chapel and another the old oak tree near the cemetery and soon the storm obliterated the sun and turned the day to night.

And still the Rain Maker prayed.

For an hour he prayed in the pouring, driving rain.

Finally the initial fury of the storm subsided and a steady rain fell on the town and the surrounding land. The Rain Maker got to his feet and smiled. He looked to the heavens and in that smile thanked them.

He picked up the soaked carpetbag placing the book into it and walked back to the hotel. His hat, boots and long coat were drenched but strangely his suit and shirt seemed to be totally dry.

The townsfolk were now celebrating in the saloon and the beer flowed like the rainwater that continued to teem down onto that small town on the plains.

The Rain Maker walked into the saloon and in the door said, "I must go. I have other work to do. I must leave. I have come for my payment."

The mayor rushed forward, shook his hand and slapped him on the back. He smiled the same treacherous smile that he had smiled earlier.

"We all want to thank you son," the mayor said toasting him with whiskey, "you've done a fine job! Frankly amazing sir! Amazing! Hell son, we've got rain enough so it will never stop!"

Then dipping into his pocket he said, "But, well, we are a poor town and figure five dollars is all we can afford to give you," and he pressed five coins into his hand.

Around him the townsfolk, heady with drink and celebration, agreed, "Not bad for an hour's work boy! It's more than enough reward! It will pay for your hotel and a good meal once you get to the next town."

The Rain Maker looked at the dusty tarnished coins in his hand and counted them neatly, one by one, onto the bar then pushed them away.

"Well," he sighed, "it is not the first time. It will not be the last time. But you have made your choice. And now you must live with its consequences", and he picked up his carpet bag and disappeared through the saloon doors into the muddy street.

As he went the town's folk jeered him and agreed amongst themselves that he had just been lucky. A few magic tricks and prayer could not bring the rain! There must have been a storm brewing anyway. But the Rain Maker knew differently. He walked down Main Street and the rain washed through his long hair. He walked down Main Street and out of the town dissolving like a spirit into the lashing rain of the storm that deluged the town.

The next morning the sun did not rise over One Horse and still it rained. It rained on the fields and on the farms and still it rained. It rained on the streets and the saloon. And it rained. It rained on the houses and the roofs. And it rained.

The next day came and went and the next and the next and still it rained. The town had had enough rain but still it rained. The roofs leaked and roads became impassable.

The fields became waterlogged and formed lakes washing the crops away and turning the meadows into infertile swamps and rancid marshes. The streets became thick muddy rivers that seeped in to flood the houses, the store, the saloon and the hotel.

For forty days and forty nights it rained until the town of One Horse was washed from the once fertile plain as if it had never existed. The rain drowned the fields and the farms. Those few buildings that were still standing rotted where they stood. Nature had taken back what was hers.

At dawn on the forty-first day the rain ceased as if a tap had suddenly been turned off. Only a handful of citizens stayed in One Horse and saw the sun rise on that day.

And they regretted not paying the Rain Maker for his work, regretted not asking him to stay and wished they could have stopped the rain he had started.

For the Rain Maker had nature as an ally.

For the Rain Maker had right on his side.

For the Rain Maker kept his word.

Uncharted Lands

We lived in uncharted lands,
Explored as children hand in hand
We saw so far, we reached so tall,
We built on sand, we were doomed to fall
Were you with me in those summer days,
Your eyes of beauty, through the haze
Do they watch me through the night,
Hunting, waiting until they bite
Wrapped around you in the dark,
Senses noises the ears do mark
Silence loud as booming guns,
Wakens green and grizzly ones
Flashing clock alarms my sleep,
Pray the Lord my love to keep
Ashes and echoes, ghosts that last,
How long will those memories haunt the past
Bright light comes and meets the dawn,
Taste of bitter cold damp morn'
Wisdom comes too late when young,
Songs of joy are seldom long
The higher they stand the further they fall,
We should have never reached so tall
We loved in those uncharted lands,
Lost and abandoned hand in hand.

The Squonk

"So often we spend our whole life chasing our dreams.
How often do we catch them only for a moment,
And then see them dissolve like tears in the rain..."

It was a dark and stormy night... No! It really was a dark and stormy night. The rain had been lashing down like stair-rods for hours and the ground was flooded and marshy. The wind whistled round the eaves of the tavern and rattled the shuttered windows. Inside the fire crackled and spluttered in the hearth sending ashes scurrying up the chimney to safety.

The landlord wiped down the bar with a dirty old rag and mopped up the puddles of beer. Hackett, the old village butcher, sat near the fire warming his bones and nursing a mug of cheapest ale. He stared into the fire and watched the embers dance and play.

Suddenly, the silence was broken by the tavern door flying open. There, framed in the doorway was a hunter. His wet feathered hat was pulled down over his face and his long green coat was soaked and dripped on the threshold. In his belt was a brace of pheasant and a wood pigeon. In his one hand he carried a wet and rusted gun and in his other a damp sack.

He walked into the warmth and kicked the door behind him with his foot and it slammed shut. He threw the gun and sack onto the nearest table and sat down exhausted, removing his hat. At the bar the landlord poured him ale and placed it gently before him.

The hunter looked up through his bedraggled black hair with tired eyes. The landlord could see they were wild as if he had seen a ghost.

"I had him!" the hunter said, "I had him" he repeated and as if to emphasise his frustration he slammed his fist on the table spilling an inch of the beer. He gazed apologetically at what he had done and mopped the spillage with the empty sack.

"What have you seen?" the landlord asked.

"Seen?" the hunter said smiling, "Not just seen, man! I had him! In this sack. I had him!"

The landlord could see the hunter clutched the sack tightly with his left hand.

"I got him!" the hunter said, "I'd caught the Squonk!" and he lifted the ale in toast to himself.

The landlord picked up the nearest stool and sat down, "and what is a Squonk?" he asked.

Leaning forward and indicating the landlord should do the same, the hunter told his story.

"Ten year ago I first heard it. Sobbing away to itself. A sad creature by all accounts - alive at both ends but a little dead in the middle, if you get my drift. I'd followed it for days through the forest.

Finally, got in close and there it was sitting on a rotten tree stump. Sobbing like a baby, holding a big red handkerchief to its eyes and crying into it, it was."

"So, what does it look like?" the landlord asked.

"Well, difficult to describe. Not really flesh, nor fish, nor bone." The hunter seemed to ponder for a while, "About yea big" and he raised his hand above the floor indicating something around a foot and a half tall. "Colour of wet sand. Sort of, looks like a big skinny mole or a shrew with its pointed nose but stands on its hind legs. Big sad eyes, long twitchy whiskers and a long rat-like tail."

"Did you catch it?"

"No!" the hunter said shaking his head, "Not then, it seemed to just disappear. Disappeared into thin air. Took me another ten years to finally track it down. Easy to follow mind you. Leaves a trail of little foot prints and tiny puddles of tears."

The hunter stopped for a moment taking a big swig of ale. "I finally caught up with it earlier this night. It was just sunset and the sky was glowing red and gold and orange. I'd heard it sniffling away to itself and followed the sound."

Getting in close there it was sitting on a log, sobbing and wailing occasionally. I crept up behind it, stealth-like. I watched it for a few minutes until its sobs subsided and it seemed to doze off. Then tricking it by throwing a stone to distract its attention, I rushed in and grabbed it! It wriggled and squirmed and squirmed and wriggled but I managed to get it into this old sack and tied up the top nice and tight."

"So where is it?" the landlord asked shrugging his broad shoulders.

"Oh! You may ask, my friend. You may ask!" and the hunter seemed agitated.

"I picked up the sack and threw it over my shoulder to make my way home. In the sack the creature seemed to stop wriggling and began to sob again. Quietly at first."

"Oh please mister, let me go, please, please let me go!" the Squonk said in its very squeaky voice.

"No! Never!" I shouted, "I've got you now! You'll never get away." and with that the creature began sobbing again.

"Ach, be quiet," I said, "stop your noise!" but the Squonk just seemed to wail even louder.

"But please mister, let me go, please, please, please, please, please let me go!" the Squonk pleaded.

"No! Never! Ever!" I said, "and I clutched the sack tighter on my shoulder. Again the sobbing was even louder. Then suddenly it stopped. It was silent. Not a sound. I put down the sack, which had seemed to become lighter and hurriedly untied the top. I opened it up and peered inside. The sack was empty. Completely empty. Except. Well, there in the bottom was a pool of bubbles and tears. Just a pool of tears!"

The landlord stared in amazement at the hunter, "Gone?" asked the landlord.

"Gone", replied the hunter.

At the hearth Hackett looked up from his fire watching and said, "So you saw it did ye?" the old man smiled, "Saw the Squonk!" and he chuckled to himself.

The hunter and landlord looked over to where the old man warmed his bones.

"But how did it escape?" the landlord asked.

"Ah!" the old man smiled, a toothless grin, It was just a trick of the tail," he said wagging a boney finger at them, "just a trick of the tail."

Outside the rain lashed down on the roof and the wind whistled through the trees, but over all the noise of the storm you could just hear the sound of a gentle sobbing.

Under the Desert Moon

We played like reckless children, under the desert moon
We rocked and rolled in freedom, under the desert skies
  That single star that shimmered, under the desert moon
  The sound of sand that's shifting, under the desert skies

We were barefoot in the sand, under the desert moon
We were walking heart in hand, under the desert skies
  Sunset turned to violet, under the desert moon
  Souls were born again, under the desert skies

We tamed the raging stallions, under the desert moon
We rode the wave of heat, under the desert skies
  Desert roses blooming, under the desert moon
  A hint of sandalwood, under the desert skies

We dreamt of quieter summers, under the desert moon
We talked of better ways, under the desert skies
  Warmed by dune blown breezes, under the desert moon
  Rivers burst from the barren, under the desert skies

We watched the candles flicker, under the desert moon
We watched the stars fall, under the desert skies
  Slept and dreamt of summers, under the desert moon
  Woke refreshed again, under the desert skies

We held each other closer, under the desert moon
We danced like chiffon soft, under the desert skies
  Questions at once were answered, under the desert moon
  Making love under our star, under the desert skies

The Hermit

"No man is an island they say but many try to be."

Once upon a time there lived a hermit. The hermit was old but though he had seen many years and many things he was not very wise. He had once lived down in the valley in the village but had got so fed up with all the things that were going wrong, people coming in from other villages to live, new roads, new buildings and so much change he just could not put up with it. He had decided that it would be better to live on top of the mountain so that he could look down on the village and glower or perhaps throw a few rocks down on it whenever he felt like.

He had once had a wife, children and even grandchildren and though they had been infinitely patient with his temper tantrums, moods and selfishness, one day he had come home to find his dinner uncooked and that, he had said, had been the final straw. He packed a huge knapsack and stomped up the mountain. Shouting back insults and shaking a fist as he went.

The top of the mountain was not a palace but it had everything he needed; animals he could trap, plants, nuts and berries he could eat and wood he could burn. It also had caves which, though very damp, he could shelter in and call home. There was even a small tarn in which he could fish when he needed to think and catch trout to eat.

During the day he would either fish, gather wood or food, make hot tea from the leaves or do crossword puzzles to pass the time. At night he would light a fire and cook a trout over it and stare down at the twinkling lights of the village in disgust.

"So much wasted wood on stupid lights," he would think.

He would sit and "harrumph" at the villagers' decadence and turn around on the rock he was sitting so that he had his back to them.

More than anything he liked a really good moan about things.

He would moan about being too hot or too cold, about the rain or the sunshine, about the food, about the incomers to the village, about the rocks being too hard, the clouds being too white or the sky not being blue enough.

He found the more he moaned the more angry he got with things and the better he felt so the more he would moan and the more angry he would get next time.

One day he was sitting drinking tea and doing a crossword puzzle and wondering whether he should do a spot of fishing when he heard someone coming up the track from the village. It was a young man, carrying a large knapsack and whistling as he went.

As he approached, the man waved at him, "Goooood morning!" he said.

"Is it?" the hermit asked sarcastically.

"Oh yes, I believe it is. The sun is shining and the wind is whispering through the trees."

"Well, I wish the sun were cooler and the wind didn't blow so much. Doesn't do my old bones any good."

The man smiled and dropped his bag by the fire, "Well, wish then and see if it makes any difference."

"It won't!" the man replied.

"Of course not. So what's the point for wishing for something you can't have? Better to wish for something you can surely?"

The hermit ignored him and said, "Just a minute. What are you doing here?"

"I've come to try out being a hermit."

"Well you can't do it here. You can't have two hermits on one mountain! It's not right. You wouldn't be a hermit then would you?"

"Well, I don't know of any rule against it. Besides, I thought I could learn from you."

"Well you can't."

The man looked at him for a moment then smiled, "Wait a moment," and he wagged his finger at the hermit, "this is a test isn't it? You old dog you…"

"No it isn't a test! I just value my privacy."

"Value your privacy? No, you can't fool me. Look I'll take that cave over there and I'll have a quick nap before supper."

"Quick nap before supper!" the hermit said in exasperation, "you can't stay. GO AWAY!" But the man just smiled and carrying his knapsack, walked into the cave said, "I know you. You old dog."

The hermit was left with hands on hips tutting and stamping his feet. "Quick nap. Supper. Indeed!" he muttered to himself and stomped off to do a crossword.

Some hours later just as the sun began to set the man awoke and with a huge yawn came out of the cave scratching his backside. He looked down at the village with the lights as they twinkled into life and a fire of the sunset as it began to glow on the horizon.

"Wow," exclaimed the man, "that's a beautiful sight! It's no wonder you stay up here."

Again the hermit tried to ignore him. "So, what's for supper?"

"Supper! You'll get no supper from me. I've got a nice trout and you're not having any!" the hermit said.

"Hey," the young man said very impressed, "you're very good at this hermit being miserable thing aren't you?" Again silence from the hermit except a glower, "…well not to worry." The man said shrugging his shoulders, "I've got some steak and eggs in my knapsack. I quite fancy that. Mmmm…"

An hour later the young man sat with his back against a rock watching the village's twinkling lights and his hands on his belly. Meanwhile, the hermit sat with his back to him doing a crossword.

"Mmm... That was tasty," the young man said stretching, "You know I could really get used to this hermitting life. So. How long have you been a hermit?"

"Nearly a week," the hermit said.

"Just a week! So at the moment it's more of a sulk than a long-term hermitting thing?" the man asked smirking.

Again, silence. "You used to live in the village didn't you?"

"Yes. And…" the hermit said gritting his teeth and wanting to be alone.

"Well it's just that you don't seem to be missed very much."

"What do you mean?"

"Well, I met your wife on the way up the hill. Nice woman. Gave me the steak and eggs. She said to me, 'if you want to spend your days with a moaning-faced old misery on you go. I'm glad rid of him' she said."

"She said that?"

"Absolutely. Said she was happy to be rid of your miserable face and was off to the village dance tonight to find a new husband."

"Dance! We never go to dances."

"You never go to dances. She seems to like them."

"The mayor said that the village was a happier place without you too."

"The mayor? He was a good friend I thought."

"Seems not. Said you moaned from morning to night and only stopped when you were asleep. You were about as much fun to have around as a rabid dog he said."

"I wasn't moaning! I was only pointing out the faults and problems in the world," the hermit said trying to explain.

"Sounds the same thing to me."

"Right!" the hermit said getting to his feet. "I'll show them!"

"Wait a moment. Where are you going?" the man said.

"The village. I'm going to..."

"You can't. You're banned. The mayor said to tell you that you can only return on certain conditions."

"But... but... they let anyone into the village. Anyone."

"Anyone with something to contribute. To give and better the village. Not to take away or steal."

"I don't steal!!" the hermit said indignantly.

"You steal every good moment from everyone's life. You steal the energy, the happiness of the moment, the beauty from people's life."

"And frankly I don't blame them for not wanting you back. You know they've even passed a law. It's called 'Moaning Without Due Cause'. Do you know that?"

"What... What should I do?"

"Well if you enjoy being alone and miserable and a moaning-faced old misery I'd stay where you are if I were you. You are obviously very good at it." Then getting to his feet the young man said, "If not I would begin by saying sorry."

"I never realised what it would do to people."

"No. You didn't... or me," the man said.

"You? What do you mean you?" the hermit asked.

"You don't know me do you?"

"No. I met you for the first time just a few hours ago."

The young man smiled, "I am you! I'm your inner child. The youth, goodness and innocence in you. The thing that sees the beauty and truth in life. God's work and infinite love. Mind you I'm not surprised you didn't know me, I've had to grow up a little to survive."

The hermit looked into the young man's eyes and saw the truth in them at which a tear began to form and rolled down the hermit's cheek, "...I'm sorry..., very sorry. I didn't realise how awful I was to be around. I'm very, very sorry," he said.

The young man smiled and placed his hands on the hermit's shoulders and said, "Well, that's a good start..."

So the hermit packed up his knapsack and threw it over his shoulder ready to return to the village. "Will you come with me?" he asked.

"Of course; whenever you need me I'm always there if only you ask...," the young man said, and he placed a finger on the hermit's heart.

So the hermit said goodbye to the young man and journeyed back down the mountain track and what happened next you can only imagine.

He walked straight to the village hall. The dancing stopped and the hermit climbed onto the stage and apologised for his moaning and vowed never to moan again on pain of imprisonment.

For three months after the villagers and his family put the man on parole. Sure enough the man never moaned or was a misery again. And in fact people began to gather at his house and enjoy his jokes and his company.

And occasionally when he had an afternoon to spare he would climb back up the mountain and talk with the young man and together they would watch the beauty of the sunset and the lights of the twinkling village as they washed into the azure evening.

A Candle in the Dark

You are the morning, you are the day
You are the sunshine, you are the way
    You are the dawning, you are the light
    You are the warming, you are the night

You are the angel, you are the white
You are the reading, you are the write
    You are the starburst, you are the glow
    You are the moonlight, you are the flow

You are the thunder, you are the fight
You are the rhythm, you are the right
    You are the river, you are the flow
    You are the arrow, you are the bow

You are the blue sky, you are the glow
You are the fields, you are the meadow
    You are the wonder, you are the why
    You are the wisdom, you are the wise

You are the heaven, you are the earth
You are the dying, you are the birth
    You are the silence, you're from above
    You are the peace, you are the love

And the light shines on, and we all watch in wonder
And the light shines on, a candle in the dark
    And the light shines on, and we listen to the thunder
    And the light shine on, a candle in the dark

When and If...

When you've left a trail of destruction
And there not a single bridge to burn
If you've smashed up all of the barriers
And you've run out of earth worms to turn

When you've wounded the enemy with needles
And you've jabbed at their heart with a word
If you've left them dying and bleeding
And you've realised your pen's not a sword

You'll be left with your conscience as comfort
You'll be left with your babblings to brook
You'll be left with an open heart bleeding
And be given that withering look

So before you go throwing you weight around
So before you lob in that grenade
Remember the destruction you've wrought
When your debt to revenge has been paid

Tales to Tell

There is no music, no poem, no song, nor story
No day, no night, no sun, nor rain
No picture, painting, past or present
Can show my heart, my love, my life
In all its wonder, joy and smiles
Of future, truth and happy times
In loving arms my soul is given
And living love my life with yours
For all the many days to come
For all the nights in warmth we'll sleep
When troubled waters seem to rise
I'll calm the restless stormy times
With strong arms and soft words
And warmth and softer kisses
So music, poem, song and story
Is played, and read and sung and told
As will be our future life together
A couple, two as one should be

A Breath Away

A soft still evening as reds and coral gather at dusk
England rests as the cool breeze bends the willow
From my window, a lawn of green lines daisied and flowered borders
A garden of Browning, Keats, Shakespeare and Wordsworth
Such beauty sleeps too, but far away in colder highlands
Golden, fair and blue like childhood summer days
Wrapped in warm eider and down, hugging a pillow as I hug mine
Sighing our happiness, as one, we'll sleep and dream together
Holding each other's hearts in lambs wool, warm and precious
My angel and I, reaching out to touch our stars in sleep.

The Long March

Tattered flags are flying, battered men to rest
Failed the final curtain, failed the ultimate test
Gone and long forgotten, evil has not won
Triumph for the future. A final battle begun!

Short Memories

I Cannot See You, They Cannot Try.
We Shall Forget You, Until We Die.
He is Now with You, I Will Be Soon.
Singing an Anthem - a Glorious Tune.

The Rest is Silence

"To be or not to be, That is the question.
... or journey to that undiscovered country"

It had been one of those summer's days, which lives in the heart like a glowing ember and sparks the soul in the winter of discontentment. His spirit glowed with love for his life and his wife.

His life had touched many and those that he had known had had one crisis or another, like a sudden storm that hits without warning, to navigate through. It seemed to be an ubiquity of modern living. He and his wife, however, had been lucky, perhaps even charmed, and through 15 years of marriage they had found contentment. Perhaps the pain of their previous disastrous relationships had been a reminder of the consequence of failing in this one.

His wife joined the short queue for a copy of the programme and he stood at the bar sipping a dry champagne. His left hand dipped into his inside jacket pocket and took out the tiny envelope. He broke the seal and poured its powdery contents into the slender glass. The champagne fizzed and effervesced, greeting the substance angrily.

He turned and raised the glass to the giant black-and-white photograph of Laurence Olivier that hung over the bar and toasted the great man. Then with one sour gulp he drunk the liquid down and he felt it trickle coldly down his throat and into his stomach.

He felt an arm around his shoulder and a squeeze from his wife as she returned. She looked at the empty glass, "Drunk it already! Another? Yes?"

"Sure. Yes. Let's have another, we're not driving are we!" and he ordered two glasses of dry white German hock.

As the barmaid passed them two golden glasses his wife said excitedly, "I promise I'll complete the last chapter of the manuscript tonight before I go to bed. So far it has been riveting. Your best yet. I can't wait to see what happens to the author!"

"It's okay! Sweetheart!" he replied, "Don't worry. You've got plenty of time to complete it!"

The play thus far had been magnificent but then "Hamlet" was one of their favourite Shakespeare's. Done well and it was inspiring. Done badly and it was painful. They had seen it many times in a variety of venues, styles, periods and casts and each time they had gathered some new nuance or sub-text previously hidden.

The day too had been a success. They had shopped in the town and visited Shakespeare's Birthplace. They had gorged on cream tea, taken a short walk on the river to look at the canal barges and then after dinner had mingled with the audience as they had gathered for the performance. Their front of centre circle seats gave them a panoramic view of the action.

He had always found an affinity with Hamlet. His own character was essentially one of a destructive nature but it had been tamed by his wife's understanding and balanced spirit. He found himself to be occasionally cynical and bitter - a trait inherited from his father but his wife was able to see the positive and good in everything. As he had watched the first act of the tragedy unfold he seemed to notice a trait in Hamlet's character he had not noticed before - one that had become clear to him that related to his own destiny - he felt that Hamlet's final demise was inevitable.

His mind wandered back to the previous summer and the day he had visited his doctor for the results of various tests he had after a bout of sudden dizziness. The doctor broke the news with ineptitude and as the months went on he realised that he had accelerated decrepitude. Some mornings his body ached and eventually he knew his mind would follow into a pitiful descent. He could not face such a prospect and could not bear to see his wife having to suffer his indignities either. He would free them both of the inevitable burden.

Since he had learnt the news he had lived life and experience to extremes. They had finally done their round-the-world tour and the holidays they had dreamed of. He had the finances in order so his wife would be stable.

They celebrated their 15th anniversary with friends in style. As the days passed he knew that time was ebbing away from them. They had savoured so much in the past months but he knew that the end was close. It was as if he was working through a hand-over of his life. With that complete he felt that now he was ready. Now he was prepared.

When he had been unable to stand or grip a cup or bear the pain he had reassured his wife that he had been drunk or over-tired or having a bad day – perhaps she believed him, he was unsure.

"Are you OK?" she asked, "you seemed miles away!"

"Sorry," he replied composing himself, "just thinking about the day. It has been wonderful. Memorable. I've really enjoyed it!" and he gripped her hand tightly.

She smiled at him knowing there was perhaps more to what he was saying but he could not articulate it. He reached into his jacket and handed her a small blue velvet box.

"This is for you, "he said, "I just wanted to say I love you…"

She opened it and revealed a sapphire and emerald eternity ring. She stared at his eyes that seemed to almost well with emotion and in the noise of the bar they kissed. It was a kiss that only they could know the meaning of and a kiss that could not be written.

The warm embrace was broken gently by the noise of the bell for Act 2. He took her hand and led her back to their seats.

As the second Act began he thought about the letter he had received earlier in the week from the publisher confirming the agreement of the publishing contract. He had remembered how he thought it would be another rejection letter but the contract offered £150,000 for his trilogy over three years with an advance of another £50,000. The cheque had been in his pocket ever since – he smiled when he thought of how his English schoolteacher had said he had no talent to write!

The lights dimmed and the actors took the stage. Hamlet's return from England and Ophelia's burial had a certain significance. The story weaved toward the inevitable duel with Hamlet and Laertes.

As the final scene played out its terrible events he thought about how he had kept the final chapter he had written a secret from his wife. If she had read it she would have perhaps guessed his actions. In his book the hero, an author, dies watching "Hamlet".

With his mind growing easier he watched the action almost from above. It seemed so ordered and inevitable. He held his wife's hand throughout the final scene and felt himself become gradually drowsy. He felt himself lifted high above the audience and the action that played itself out. The drugs had softened the pain of departure and he drifted into slumber, his life dimming like the bright beacon of light he was drawn to.

And as the prince was taken to his peace, "The Rest was Silence".

Thinking Of…

We met as through the grace of time,
My heart was yours and yours was ever mine
We thought that all the world was ours
We could sit and chase the wandering clouds for hours
Our lives wrapped like summer flowers as one
Days were warm and the meadows green and sunned
How could these everlasting days find end
As we watched the twinkling stars above
So, what was it we were thinking of?

We saw the sun rise on the Taj at dawn
And the canyons, the rivers and those French fields of corn
We saw the pyramids rise from out the desert sands
And the streams of the summer flowing through our hands
We saw the mountains of ice rise into the sky
And the castles of dreams that would live and ever die
We saw the sun beat down on every bright new day
And we thought we'd always find away
So, what was it we were thinking of?
Please tell me, what was it we were thinking of?

Now time has passed and the blessed dove has flown
We stay as friends and think of all that we once owned
A warmth will live in the corners of our soul
What remains will always leave a hole
And I dream of those sun-filled glory times
Given to us by the grace of the divine
I remember how we would sit and watch the sun
You and I were single and the one.
We said they would never end our love
So, what was it we were thinking of?

Let Love, Hope and Innocence Prevail

*"So many have died in the name of religion, governments and nations.
For flag and a rag on a pole. For money, greed and wealth.
Ah! So much has been lost."*

They had long forgotten why the war was being fought, something about land and flags and lines on a map, something they could not wholly understand but the misery and suffering that the war brought seemed to be all around them.

The war had raged beyond their borders for more than a year and they had always believed, perhaps vainly, that it would never touch them. At the opening of spring, when the flowers struggle to bloom through the hard frosty earth there was a fresh push by the enemy and the battle entered their land.

Through the winter, as the lovers held each other for comfort in front of the warm fire, they had talked around this eventuality, never believing it would ever become a stark and cold reality. They knew that as the battle got ever closer he would have to leave and stand and fight, to defend his life and loves.

His respected position in the village gave him the rank of captain and the command of a hundred souls who she knew he would protect as his children - no life would be lost for vanity or glory. Her husband, for all intents an ordinary man, was certainly no warrior but when needs must she always knew he would fight to protect land, home and wife.

They loved each other as no others they knew. He lit up like the sun in the winter when she entered the room and she knew he felt the same, the warmth in his heart shone through his dark brown eyes.

On the night before he left they made love until the morning light broke through the window.

Until the last moment they were wrapped in each other's arms impressing the smell, the touch, the taste, the warmth and kiss of each other into their memories like a photograph.

The day he went away, he arose and prepared himself while she still slept. He saddled his white horse; he dressed in his officer's uniform and ate a hearty breakfast. She came downstairs wrapped in a thick gown and he stood before her in the hall in his uniform, polished boots, spurs and long coat.

As he mounted his horse he kissed her hand tenderly and they exchanged a glance that spoke a thousand sonnets and a volume of words. They knew they would see each other again. They knew it.

"Let love, hope and innocence prevail my Love...." he said and she smiled as his hand slipped softly from hers and he spurred his horse away.

The rest of that first day they were apart was dark and dank and seemed to last a month. When she went to bed it had always been her habit to leave the curtains open to catch the dawn light and so on the window ledge she placed a large candle which she lit as a beacon to shine across the valley and, one day, call him home.

"Let love, hope and innocence prevail, my Husband..." she whispered under her breath.

The long days turned to weeks which drifted into months. As time would allow she would receive a letter from him full of sweet words and news of his triumphs. All the news seemed to be good and it seemed as if the war would be ended before autumn turned to winter.

One night as she locked and barred the doors, she looked over the garden to the valley and could see dark storm clouds gathering on the horizon. It would be a rough night.

She climbed the stairs and, as every night, lit the candle and closed her eyes as she kissed her husband good night in her thoughts remembering again his warmth and touch.

As the night wore on the candle danced and fluttered in the window, creating dark monstrous shadows on the walls and ceiling. She pulled the covers around her head and eventually drifted into a restless sleep.

And in her dreams she dreamt she was standing on the steps to their house looking over the valley. It was as if she could see far and away and for miles. Across the valleys, across the hills and mountains, over the river and streams she saw her husband.

He was riding his beautiful white horse and he rode ahead of his men commanding a regiment of cavalry. Their swords were held limply at their sides and glinted golden in the autumn sunlight. The horses walked slowly forward, at first slowly then into a canter. The riders rose in the saddle and spurred their mounts forward and the canter became a trot and then a furious gallop. A blistering gallop now, leaning along the steed's neck with swords in the air, towards the unseen enemy.

Then cannon fire began to explode around the charging line of men as they screamed a frightening battle cry, their horses wide-eyed in fear.

Then her dream when into dreadful slow motion with her husband galloping towards her. There was an explosion; a shell burst in front of him, felling the horse and it rolled broken in the dust. Its rider lay close by as other riders charged passed their fallen leader oblivious to his injury. As the dust cleared she could see that he lay next to his fallen horse, motionless. Inert. Blood trickled from a wound at his side and his dark hair was stained with his life.

In her dream she was panic stricken. She rushed to his side and knelt in the dust in an eerie silence.

"...Not this way, not this way...," she prayed for his life.

She reached out to touch him, did he live?

She woke with a start...

She realised that she was sobbing and that the room was now dark, the candle, her beacon to him had been snuffed out by the storm.

She got out of bed wrapping the quilt around her for warmth. She rushed to the window and looked into the darkness. The storm had abated and she desperately relit the candle, which seemed to refuse to light and she cursed it in the darkness.

As the candle once again gave out light she heard a frantic hammering on the front door and a voice calling her.

She ran down the stairs almost tripping in her gown and unlocked the door frenetically.

At the door was a stranger, an old soldier, blood stained and dusty, a warhorse panting and agitated behind him.

"Madam, I have ridden many days to find you. My commander sent me. Our captain, you husband, was wounded in a great cavalry charge. His life hangs by a thread and we know not if he will live or die. He calls out your name in his fever and restlessness."

Without hesitation she turned to leave.

"Madam, wait. Where do you go?"

"To dress myself and saddle my horse."

"Madam. That cannot be! The road is long and hard, the journey difficult and dangerous and I could not guarantee your safety."

She laughed out loud in a mocking tone. "May love, hope and innocence prevail sir! In this I am fearless. I will, nevertheless, no matter what the dangers, accompany you to my husband's side."

Within an hour, with the officer barely rested, they were back on the road. As the journey wore on, the terrible sights she saw, the smell of death in her nostrils and the destruction of her lands made her weep with pity and sadness.

The old soldier told her how her husband had led a great cavalry charge, which had routed the enemy. They both learnt that only a few days after he had left the front the enemy had capitulated. Peace was returning to their land and the men were beginning to return to their homes and families at last.

Some days later they arrived in a small village in the south of their country and at an old farmhouse with a long barn which was barely standing but which nevertheless had been turned into a makeshift hospital.

Without tethering her horse she leapt from the saddle and ran into the barn. Inside along each wall were the wounded and the dying. Nurses comforted the dying holding cold hands in the last moments.

Then she saw him. At first she thought she was too late, he lay as motionless as she had last seen him in his dream.

Then he moved his hand across his body. She knelt beside him and taking his hand kissed it.

In his dream he seemed to smile, then spoke. It was barely audible.

"My love. My life," he said.

Then she felt a hand on his shoulder. It was a doctor.

"Madam. You should not have come. These sights are not for your eyes."

"Sir, I am my husband's wife. It is my duty. I would be not be my husband's wife if I had not."

He smiled and shook his head. "Well. He's through the worst, God knows how. We thought he had died a few days ago, his breath was imperceptible. But his inner strength seems to have saved him. He will live but his convalescence may be long."

"As long as the tides turn and the sun shines I will care for him," she replied.

As the gathering dusk became a crystal clear moonlit night she sat at his side, stroking his hand and comforting him. A nurse, her uniform torn and stained with blood, walked to the window opposite the bed and lit a candle which guttered in the breeze.

"He seemed to sleep easier when this candle was lit," she said.

The lady smiled in wonder and thanked her and then said "When we first met, my husband taught me a poem that I should remember and repeat in the darkest of hours. It goes:

May Love, Hope and Innocence Prevail!
May Love, Hope and Innocence Prevail!
Believe that Love will Never Fail.
May Love, Hope and Innocence Prevail!"

Then she placed her head on his chest and listened to his heart beating softly. As she did so he gently raised his hand and placed it on her head and stroked her hair and soon they slept together once more.

All That I Am

I lie awake some mornings, while you're sound asleep
Listening to you breathing, imaging your dreams so deep
And as I lie in your warmth, wrapped around, of course,
I think of our adventures; our quest to find the source
Of slaying countless dragons and building bridges wide
Of finding shining castles and stemming the restless tides
Of how we've climbed those mountains and discovered foreign lands
Of how each daily step has been together, ever hand in hand
And I will always try to be, your knight in armour shining
But I know I'm not always light and see the silver lining
And when perhaps I have stumbled, or tripped with heavy bane
You've caught me in your arms and made me whole again
How I think of you each moment, every second of every day
Of your love, of being together, as we fight to find the way
How every kiss brings purpose to your humble man
As I strive to be your husband, to be better than I am
How each and every smile from your loving face
Brings me to my heart of hearts and leads me to that place
Where you and I are one, as soul mates together in life
A single pulse of golden light as one as man and wife
So, sweetest love, when you see me as you do
Remember, I am, all that I am; and all that I am is you.

Mr Time

"We're hopelessly working in line
For what we can see or can't find.
Hopelessly working in time
For what we can't know or won't find."

It was, to say the least, a very special gift. He had been given it because of his job and moreover his long and faithful services to hard work which, judging by the number of mild heart attacks he had suffered, was considerable. It was only a matter of time before he would suffer a major one.

During his short 45-year lifetime, from the age of 20, he had taken just one week vacation, at his wife's insistence, when he had done absolutely nothing - no walking, canoeing, skiing, mountain biking, just nothing - lying by a pool with just his wife, a book and a towel for company.

Now, in celebration of his hard work and his other considerable achievements he sat in a room waiting to be ushered through to meet and interview the man he had fought against, snatching just a few victories, all his life. He was not nervous, just a little apprehensive, and wondered what this man would be like.

Rather than waste time he took out his laptop and checked his diary for the rest of the week. Not many gaps. Phew! Lots to do.

Then, as if by magic, the door on the opposite walk opened wide, beckoning him to enter. He rose from the sofa and walked across the room and through the door.

The room was full, from floor to ceiling with clocks. Big ones, small ones, grandfathers, grandmothers, carriage, chiming, kitchen, mantel piece, self-winding, perpetually ticking clocks. There was not an inch of wall space without a timepiece. The room was carpeted with a clock pattern, the curtains a deep lush red, decorated with roman numerals.

In a large rocking chair in the bay window gazing out of the window was a middle-aged man, humming to himself.

The man turned and smiled and said, "Come on my boy, come on, don't dawdle, hurry now, take a seat." He did so and sat opposite him on a seat built into the bay window.

"So. What do you want to ask?" the old man asked, "What would you ask of Mr Time?"

"Firstly, thanks for agreeing to see me - your time must be very valuable."

"Oh, it is," said Mr Time firmly, "as is everyone's of course." And he leant over and touched the man's arm and winked.

"Of course, of course. How old are you?"

Mr Time shrugged, "Not sure really. Someone once said time is relative. I just know I've seen many things and that I don't seem to be getting older very quickly. Perhaps I'm immortal, for a limited time."

"But, how do you stay alive if you're immortal."

"Oh that's easy. Everyone is given a limited amount of time to achieve the things they need to do. If they value time they waste very little of it. There are rules of course, how long you can spend eating, sleeping all that stuff, and how much time you need for rest, but after that if you don't value time then you're wasting it and that's where I come in."

"I don't understand," the young man said rather puzzled, doodling notes on his pad.

"Well every minute that is wasted comes to me! Where do you think those wasted moment sgo to? Look…" and reaching down to his tie he lifted it and pulled a magnifying glass from his inside jacket pocket, "…here, take a look." And he offered the young man the magnifying glass.

The young man examined the tie and on closer inspection realised the symmetrical dotted pattern he had seen was made from thousands upon thousands of tiny watches, some perfectly still, others moving, ticking their seconds away.

Mr Time smiled and lifted his jacket sleeve. The pattern slightly different, the content the same, thousands of ticking clocks.

"My clothes are all the same, I have quite a few suits like this - have them specially made of course. You see every clock belongs to someone. Every minute they waste ticks up a second on the clock."

"The more they waste, the more it shows on the clock. They waste an hour, I get a minute - you get the idea. The more I get the longer I live. Come and see this," and Mr Time ushered the young man over to one of the side walls.

"Pick a drawer." The young man chose one and Mr Time proudly slid it open for him. The drawer was full of what seemed to be diamonds sparkling against the baize. Again on inspection every one was a tiny ticking clock.

"But surely you must have lots of left-over minutes? Minutes you don't use for your life?"

"Oh yes, hours worth! Days worth! Centuries worth," Mr Time said clapping his hands, "that's the beauty of it. You've heard of the expression - 'the devil makes work for idle hands' - well it's quite literally true. I 'sell it on' if you like to the devil (nasty piece of work - wouldn't bother looking him up) and he uses it any way he likes, you know causing trouble, fights, wars, accidents, riots, death, mayhem, rape, drunkenness, all that sort of stuff."

"But that's terrible!" the young man said in exclamation flopping back and thumping the arm of the chair.

"I know, but what can I do? I've got more time on my hands than I can sensibly use and I wouldn't have so much if people didn't waste so much. That's where you come in...," and Mr Time leant forward in the rocking chair and pointed at him dramatically.

"What do you mean?" the young man asked rather puzzled.

"Well, the thing is, you've probably wasted the least time of anyone I know - I mean your clock's got just a few minutes on it I think all told, and what with people wasting less time and having busier lives I'm beginning to run a little short on time."

"I don't see how I can help or if indeed I want to."

"Well, its your choice of course, but you're a journalist. You write for a very influential newspaper and if you wrote one of your articles about how people should slow down and take things easier and all that stuff, I'm sure people would sit up and take notice."

"Mmmm, and what do I get in return?" the young man asked.

"Well, you've achieved so much already in your short life and you've almost run out of life time – the time allotted to your life – that I thought perhaps I could give you some time off for good behaviour so to speak – say ten years. You retire now. Do what you like for ten years then bang, sayonara, off to the great fluffy clouds in the sky."

"Seems a very tempting deal..."

"Oh it is. It is!" Mr Time said grinning like a Cheshire cat.

Suddenly there was an annoying warbling sound which seemed to come from Mr Time's other jacket pocket – the young man realised it was the opera bit from Bohemian Rhapsody, "I love that tune. Excuse me a moment. Mobile," and Mr Time drew a ruby encrusted phone from his jacket pocket. It was the most expensive the young man had ever seen, bright red and it shone like gold.

"Yesss, what is it?" Mr Time said impatiently, "I thought I told you never to call me when I was in a meeting?" Mr Time hissed and the young man thought for a moment that Mr Time's eyes burnt like a thousand flaming embers.

"Yes, yes, of course you can," Mr Time said condescendingly, all the while the young man could see evil and wickedness in Mr Time's face, "Look you can handle this! It's simple! Yes. Make the same deal I always make. Look. I want to see that multiple drive-by-shooting on CNN by tea time. Do you understand? Capiche!" and with that Mr Time pressed the end call button on the phone and threw it onto the side table.

The young man thought for a moment and then said, returning to Mr Time's offer, "But it seems to me the more time wasted, the more evil there would be in the world."

"Well, yes but not much more than there ever was before," said Mr Time trying to placate the situation.

Then the young man thought a while, "Can I ask another question?" Mr Time shrugged and indicated that of course he could, "What is your relationship, exactly, with the devil?"

"The devil? I don't know what you mean," Mr Time said innocently.

"Yes, the devil, the Prince of Darkness, Lucifer, 666, Fallen Angel, The Anti-Christ, The Beast, Beelzebub, the nasty guy with the horns, pitch fork and pointy tail?"

"I don't know who you mean?" Mr Time said his face the innocence of a new-born babe.

"I think you do," the young man said and with that Mr Time began to metamorphosise, changing his shape until there, before him, was the devil wearing Mr Time's suit.

The devil straightened his tie and gritted his teeth, "I will roast that stupid little demon's nethers for calling me on my mobile," and then smiling wickedly he said, "I nearly got you there though didn't I?"

"Almost, almost," and the young man got up, straightened his tie and smoothed his jacket.

"You must see that to see the good in the world there needs to be evil, surely you see that don't you?" the devil asked as the young man turned to go.

Without turning the young man said, "I think there's enough evil and wickedness on the planet without adding anymore," and with that the young man opened the door. "Goodbye," the man said closing the door behind him.

"I prefer au revoir," the devil said smiling and with a shrug he returned to his rocking chair looking out of the window onto the world.

The young man meanwhile, returned to his job, his work and what little was left of his short life, wasting as little time as possible in the time before he died. Posthumously his book, "The Devil Makes Work" was published and became an instant best seller.

The opening paragraph said:

"In this book you will find how wasting time is the root of all evil. Never waste a minute for if you do you will never know what it might be used for..."

Time and Space

When I look into the deep blue of the evening sky
And I see those million million stars
With a billion billion miles between them
And the eternity of time and space before me
I can but wonder.
I wonder of you. Of your soul and your beauty.
I wonder at the boundless, endless love we share
And I wonder how. Across those heavens,
Somewhere in time, There alone in the darkness
We could find each other
And how once two, are one,
In time and in space.
Together.

Trick of the Tail

"They've got no horns and they've got no tail
They don't even know of our existence
Am I wrong to believe in the city of gold
That lies in the deep distance"

Once upon a time... There was a handsome young man who lived ina beautiful city of gold. He was not only handsome but also rich and famous and he had but one problem. He was bored. He was bored of his life with riches and gold when he could do anything he wanted, how he wanted, whenever he wanted. He was bored with his boring life, with his boring friends, with his boring family in the boring city of gold.

So one morning he got up and instead of taking a bath in his gold bath and eating breakfast in his gold dressing gown with his gold knife and fork he threw a few things into his brand new leather knapsack and set off for adventure and to seek heaven only knows.

For he had heard of a place where people were different. Where they didn't live in golden towers but ordinary houses in ordinary towns in ordinary streets with ordinary people. Even stranger, he'd been told that these people were very different because they didn't have a long forked tail or short horns like all the other people in the golden city with golden towers.

So without telling a soul, not letting anyone know and not understanding the consequences of his actions the young man threw his knapsack over his back and set off for adventure. As he walked along the road and up the hills he walked miles and miles and the city gradually faded in the distant mist and he was very much on his own. Gone were the golden city and the golden towers he had known from childhood.

And as he walked alone on the lonely, wide and open road he dreamed of a new life and perhaps that he would meet someone and fall in love.

Someone to share in his life, someone who wasn't boring and wanted to be with him, not because he was handsome, rich and famous but because he was him.

At the end of his first day, he wrapped a coat around himself for warmth, took some soft bread from his knapsack ate it and wrapping his tail around him, settled under a giant oak tree for the night.

The next morning he awoke refreshed and full of hope and apprehension. After digging in his knapsack and breakfasting on a rapple (a strange but delicious cross between a raspberry and an apple) he set off along the open road again. He was certainly a long way from home and in the middle of nowhere.

Soon his climb turned into a down-hill lope and the countryside began to change. Gone were the familiar hills and mountains of his youth, now there were huge expanses of meadow, rivers and banks of flowers. It was truly a beautiful place to behold.

Quickly walking through the meadows he found a path and eventually the path turned into a track, which in turn became a rough road which he followed. His journey becoming easier, though still not knowing where he was going, he stepped ahead with a spring in his step and he began to whistle a happy walking tune.

Then up ahead he saw a man, walking in the opposite direction, also whistling as he walked and also having a knapsack slung over his shoulder. In every respect they were pretty much the same, well dressed, handsome and the man looked rich, but strange of strange, the man had no horns nor tail as he had been told.

He thought to himself "I'll be friendly", and as the man approached shouted, "Ho there! Good morning!"

And the man shouted back, "Good morning to you too! Travelling far?" the man asked.

"Wherever my feet will carry me – I seek adventure!" he said.

"Me also; looking for something I haven't found yet, but I'm sure I will. Anyway, I wish you well!" the man replied.

And both set off in the opposite direction with a spring in their steps not sure what they were looking for or where they would find it.

As the day wore on and the road became busy he began to meet more and more people, all without horns and tails. As he encountered each he thought, "Everyone looks so strange to me."

People had also begun to notice his strange appearance, having a tail and horns was extremely unusual – in fact unheard of, and they would ask where he was from.

He would point to the horizon and say, "I come from the great city of gold that lies off into the distance."

And they would smile and nod and nudge each other and then give each other a knowing wink then say, "I'm sure you do. Never heard of it myself," and carry on their ways chuckling to themselves.

After many day's journey he came to a small town and as he entered it everyone stared at him and pointed to his horns and his tail, they were even more surprised when he spoke.

"The stranger is strange," they said.

Then that night, while he slept under the stars in a haystack on the edge of the town, he was grabbed by the town guard and led away to the town square. At first he went with them without complaint, perhaps they wished to know more about my city of gold, he thought to himself but then he saw that a cage had been erected in the square which he was unceremoniously thrown into and he became very frightened and began to weep.

They hung a sign on the cage which read "Beast that can talk" and then left him until the morning.

The next day as soon as it was light people came from their homes to see the creature in the cage.

"Very strange," they would say, "Horns and a tail," they would sneer, "How very odd," they would say and then they would push a stick through the bars and poke at him and laugh.

At the end of the day the mayor of the town appeared.

"So creature," he said, "where did you say you were from?"

"The City of Gold, which lies in the deep distance," he replied.

"City of Gold indeed?" the mayor replied with a sneer, "What's its name?"

"We just call it City of Gold!" he replied.

"And how come you can talk?" the mayor asked.

"Have done since I was a sprog," he replied.

And putting his hand through the bars and tugging at the man's tail asked, "Is this tail real? Are those horns stuck on with glue? Are you doing this for money?"

"Yes of course they're real, we've all got horns and a tail and I don't need money!" the man replied.

"Pahh!" the mayor said and stomped off.

Some said he was a freak, some said it was a publicity stunt but after the first day everyone agreed that it was really that interesting.

So the man spent a second night in the cage and as he drifted off to sleep he made up a little song to the tune in his head which went:

They've got no horns and they've got no tail
They don't even know of our existence.
Am I wrong to believe in a city of gold
That lies in the deep distance....

And as he drifted to sleep he resolved to use his powers and to be free from his prison.

The next morning the dawn rose and he'd eaten the crust he'd been given and drunk the water, he stood at the bars and putting his hands around them and gripping one tightly in each hand he took a deep breath.

He concentrated as he had been taught and in his mind's eye visioned the bars bending as if they were butter. Beneath his hands he felt the heat and as it grew in intensity he pushed very gently and sure enough the bars opened and he marched out of the cage, free again.

And as the town folks, led by the mayor, began to gather to gawp at their catch, they saw to their surprise that their prize was free.

The young man stepped forward and grabbed the mayor by the scruff of the neck and pointing to the hills and the mountains beyond said:

"There, beyond the bounds of your weak imagination, lie the noble towers of my city, bright and gold. Let me take you there, show you a living story. Let me show you others such as me!"

And he sighed and thought of his home and his friends and the beautiful City of Gold, "Why did I ever leave my home?"

"Stories! Stories! Nothing but stories!" the mayor said.

"They are no such thing! The City of Gold shines in the morning sun, the buildings are gilded and roves trimmed with copper."

"The streets are paved with silver and lit by lamps in the night, our houses are warm and clean and comfortable. We have hot baths whenever we feel like it, fed by the warm springs," the man said, his eyes twinkling with passion in the sun light.

"Hot baths! Gold! Silver! Such nonsense!" the mayor said pointing a finger at the young man.

"Then I shall show you! I will show you!" the young man said, "I will take you there!"

During the rest of the morning they gathered an expedition party of ten or so men, with two sturdy pack horses led by the mayor and dressed in stout boots and warm woollen clothes for the journey.

Late in the morning they set off taking the road towards the green hills which led to the rough track towards the mountains and headed towards the high peak of Flattop Mountain, shrouded in wisps of clouds many miles in the distance.

For days they trudged, the climb getting steeper, the track getting rougher, the air getting thinner and each day they got closer to the peak of Flattop.

Each day the men in the party grew more despondent and each day one would disappear in the night and head home believing the journey a wild goose chase.

Finally after a week they reached the summit of Flattop Mountain which was thick with cloud. Tired and exhausted they made camp.

Around the camp fire the man told more stories of his home and as the party, that had now dwindled to only three, bedded themselves for the night they slept beginning to believe that perhaps the young man was not telling stories and that perhaps the City of Gold was not just a product of his imagination.

Very early the next morning the young man could see that the clouds were clearing and the sun was beginning to rise.

Then through the shifting clouds, far, far off on the horizon, he saw the glint of gold – his home!

"There! There!" he cried pointing to his City of Gold.

The party awoke with a start to see what the young man was so excited about.

"There! There!" he cried again pointing to the horizon.

And one of them peered through the mist and just for a moment caught a glint of gold, perhaps a spire and nodded!

"Yes!" he said, "I think I saw something".

"Ha! I told you!" the young man shouted, "Ha!" and ran down the track from Flattop towards the horizon and his home.

They called after him, "Wait! Wait!"

And as he disappeared into the mist they thought they heard him singing:

They've got no horns and they've got no tail
They don't even know of our existence
Am I wrong to believe in a city of gold
That lies in the deep distance

And they welcomed him at the gates with a shaking of hands and hugs and embraces.

"Hello friend! Welcome home."

David

When all around you light begins to soften
And greys and dark becomes a brilliant blue
A hand comes down to lead you to a heaven
Where memories warm and friends are old to you

When the pain becomes too much to bear and leadened
And life itself has lost a will to last
You leave your parents, brothers, sisters heartening
You feel a pulling warmth, a soothing blast

You have not lost the war but won a battle
Your army's tired but marches ever on
Yout smile and laughter always be remembered
David! Our brother, friend and son........

For my brother 2/2/64 to 25/9/89.

The Dreammaker

"What would it be if we could turn our dreams into reality?
What would it be if our words became actions and deeds?
My friend; we can and we do without even realising it!"

Once upon a dream there was a city like many other cities. Its people lived behind heavy iron-bolted doors nursing their fear and loathing, for it was that time. It was that time when friends were for a day, when love was lust, when music was noise, when humanity was not and when everyone dreamt of escape.

And amidst this turmoil and sterile soil sat a man in a high white tower - we'll call him Piers, a hermit of the seventh age, watching and listening to it all. He saw the hatred, he saw the envy, he could smell the violence and the fear as it rose from the streets far, far below.

Piers lived in the tall high tower, like a spindle, which rose like a finger into the sky thousands' of feet in the air, so tall, its top was a mystery, high above the city, the noise and the clouds where his only friends were the warm sun and the smiling moon.

One day as he wrote his words and listened to his music which drifted from the windows all around he heard a noise from the balcony behind him. A fluttering like that of a bird or a butterfly.

Turning he saw a beautiful faerie sitting and watching him intently. In wonder she stared at him without fear and her eyes grew wide as he smiled at her.

He, in turn, gazed at her beauty. Her hair was curled in ringlets and of a blonde that looked as though they were made of sunshine. Her skin twinkled and glittered and her eyes were of the brightest piercing electric blue. Her wings were of rainbow gossamer and twitched like a cat's tail.

He leaned forward and spoke, "You've flown a long way up to see me. What is your name?"

The faerie smiled and coyly replied, "I'm Amience; I was told you lived up here."

"Who told you?"

"Oh, it is very well known. You live high above the clouds."

"Away from the silly street folk. Away from those down there." And she pointed downwards rather indignantly.

"You don't like them?"

"Oh course not!" she said. "They don't see us. We are all around, but they don't see us. They don't hear our voices; don't see our work – not like you do."

"And where do you live?"

"We all live in the old park, down by a brook which babbles away to itself. It's quiet there now. Very quiet. We can play all day and no one disturbs us."

"Sounds wonderful."

"It is...", there was a pregnant silence as the faerie gazed around the room, then kicking her heels, she said, "...so, don't you want to know why I'm here?"

"I guess I do. "

"Well, every day and every night until very late we see your lights burning as you work on your stories. Stories which no one reads. No one. Why do you do it?"

"Because I enjoy creating magic, besides my stories are a gift."

"A gift? For whom?"

"A gift from the source to me."

"That's as may be, but no one reads them?"

"So? They are still good energy, positive magic. I have put them out into the world and perhaps a tiny piece of their essence will make a small difference to someone."

"They have."

"They have?" said the man rather surprised, "Who to? How do you know?"

"Remember, you wrote a story about the soldier who was away to war and presumed dead and his wife lit a candle and placed it in the window every night until he came home."

"And?"

"There's a woman in the city doing just that. We've seen it."

"Coincidence! There must be..."

"No just her; remember you wrote another about the man who searched the earth for the answer finding it in his lover's smile when he returned?"

"Yes? Of course… but…"

"Your stories may not be being read but they are making a difference. People are hearing your stories…"

"But how Amience, how?"

"In their sleep. Within their rest. In their dreams!"

"Impossible!"

Amience shook a finger at the man, "You know it to be the truth"

The man sank back into his chair for he knew in his heart that it was so. Through all the years he had written he'd had a feeling that his words had had a power. Thought, word and action, it was the way.

Then thinking for a moment he said, "but my ideas come from my sleep. I dream my ideas…"

"Yes, you dream your dreams, write them down and suddenly they are out there in the universe." At that the faerie pushed herself from the ledge and flew towards the man. Landing at his feet she took him by the hands.

"We've had an idea. Of how to change things for the better." And whispering into the man's ear she said, "It's simple..."

And the faerie told the man how he should write a story in which the whole city dreamt the same dream, a dream of how the city was beautiful again as in the New Age, of how people would smile and love and be loved, of how every day they would thank each other for the dawn, of how they would begin to notice the miracles of life.

With that the man turned and faced his desk. Taking out a piece of paper he placed it in readiness to write. As he did so he turned to thank the faerie but she was gone.

He took a deep breath and wrote:

Once upon a dream there was a city like any other city. Its people lived behind heavy bolted doors in a time of fear and loathing, for it was that time. It was that time when friends were for a day, when love was lust, when music was noise and when everyone dreamt of escape.

Wait a While Longer

" *Waiting for the moment*
when the moment has been waiting all the time"

There are moments in our lives when we stand at a crossroads trying to choose our next direction. Most would probably take straight on and be done with it. Some would choose the safe and well-worn path.

A few braver ones will choose the less trodden path.

Before I first met her I would have always played safe. Would have chosen the easy route, straight roads, no turns, roundabouts and no difficult navigation. Not for me the brambled way or fighting through the jungle on some quest.

When I think back on those days of mediocrity before we met it was if I had been waiting for that moment. The spark that ignites the flame, the burning ember that eventually rages into a furnace.

Once we had met, reason had no reason. Hopelessness had hope. Soul had spirit.

Like some cataclysm the whole earth stopped in its spin. Life grabbed me and shook me by the throat and begged me to deal with it.

It was love at first sight and wham! I was smitten. She was the most beautiful thing I had ever seen and I couldn't take my eyes or mind off her.

And now I sat across the table from her warming my hands on a cup of coffee.

Outside the bitter cold of winter had covered the world in a sparkling white blanket and we watched as the sun glistened on the frosty window ledge.

But, inside, even with the warmth of the log fire, I could feel her warmth glowing like an English summer's day.

She turned and smiled. Her bright sky-blue eyes touched my soul.

I had resisted her or at least I had tried. It was as much as I could do from reaching across and kissing her gently on the forehead. Something inside me had always held me back.

She smiled and lifted her drink, removing the redundant straw and placing it in the empty ashtray. She reached over and touched my hand.

"Don't worry," she said, "lessons learnt. Lessons learnt," she repeated, underlining the outcome and sipping the water.

"I could not let you love me," and she smiled into her glass, "It would have destroyed us both and others. We have to let it go..."

I knew what she was saying and understood her meaning. She was right of course, but gazing into those eyes it was impossible not to drown in them.

"But to find each other," I said, "after so long. It seems such a waste..."

"And we will find each other again," and then she thought for a moment and she said, "...maybe not today, maybe not tomorrow... but we will find each other."

I found myself tracing patterns in the spilt wine. I looked up at her again and her eyes were filling with tears.

I squeezed her cold hand. "It's okay. We have to let it go. I know you're right. You know you're right."

"This is crazy, we've only known each other a few weeks. You can't care for someone after a few weeks. It's impossible."

She seemed angry that such a thing was possible. How could two people on separate paths, from separate backgrounds, who six months before had not heard of each other, be thrown together with a force enough to change lives and question purpose? Easy. It all happens in that momentary lapse of reason that binds a life to a life. I remembered the moment again and treasured it. Even with the pain of loss I would not change a single moment.

She dipped in her coat pocket and recovered a tissue, drying her eyes. "I really have to go," she said sadly looking at her watch.

She couldn't have known what those few words did to me. I felt something reach in, squeeze my heart and then throw it into a deep black chasm. We were not young but we had been so innocent and naïve. We had never meant to break any hearts. But then again who ever does?

I looked at my watch. It was past late, "I know. We better get you back..."

We walked from the restaurant into the chill air of the car park, wrapping our coats around ourselves for warmth. Stars glistened in the night sky and the Milky Way was crystal clear. On such a night you could see forever.

She unlocked her car and turned to me looking for an answer.

"I'm sorry," I said.

"Don't be. We knew. Besides we're friends. No need," she said reassuringly.

"You know if you ever need help or a shoulder or a smile or an ear just call..." I said

"Sure..."

"You know I'm falling in love with you don't you...?"

I held her cold hands and gazing into those blue eyes for the first and only time kissed her. We held each other and her tears were warm against my cheek. The moment lasted forever and would be locked away in our hearts for as long.

Then, without another word, for none could have been said, she stepped into the car.

She started the engine and slowly drove away.

As she turned into the street she looked up from the wheel and smiled.

I don't know how long I stood in the car park watching the red tail lights disappear into the darkness. I remember feeling the tears dry on my face. I remember not feeling the cold of the night.

As I got into the car all I could think of was her warmth and her bright blue eyes that as I kissed her seemed to reflect that winter sky of stars.

And somewhere in another space an angel placed its hands on my shoulders and squeezed. Its love entered my heart and planted a thought of love and light there.

"All you need to do is look, listen and trust".

It was the ember that burns bright enough and warm enough to carry on.

One day we would meet again.

War & Peace

Breathe and let us fly regardless
Unfettered wing soar graceful and high
Borderless and blind and careless
No chain to break no knots to untie

Governments cannot protect us
Armies must stand idly by
The people shout for moral victory
But the cost of living is far too high

All at once we see the prize
End the tunnel soon the light
So he wraps his arms around us
Helps us through the endless night

Posthumous

Defiant victorious, gracious and noble
The winner? Glorious bold and reliant
Pure and defiant, cold with no future,
Warrior. Rest.

The Last Dragon of Scotland

"People believe in very strange things.
Gods and ghost and evil spirits.
They once even believed in dragons!"

Once upon a time…

Many who I meet ask what's happened to all the dragons and why don't you find dragons in Scotland?

It all began, 500 years ago in the land of Caledonia.

At that time there were many, many castles across the land. Each castle protected the people and glens around it.

Each castle was owned by a laird who had his own armies.

There is one thing that not many realise. In those days each castle had another protector. A protector more powerful than the war lords and lairds and the armies that lived in them.

For in those days each castle was watched over by a dragon. They often lived in the caves in the glens above the castles sleeping on a rocky outcrop in the bright sunshine and keeping a wary eye on the horizon and an ear open for trouble.

Now as you know dragons are usually fearsome, huge creatures. They have big wide beady eyes in green or orange and have long claws and long pointy tails. On their foreheads a true dragon has the mark of the dragon king, "Maradoc", which looks like a huge "M". Their huge mouths are full of sharp pointy teeth and if they open their mouths and hiss at you, well, beware. That's a warning that they're about to breathe fire and you wouldn't want to be close to that would you!

Well in the land of the Scots, people knew the dragons and how they protected their mountains, castles and glens and they were respected. Well, all except for one.

You see on the Isle of Arran on the Western shores of Loch Orid high in a castle on a dark granite mountain top there lived a fearsome witch called Morag. Morag and her castle had their own protector - a wicked black dragon called Mournblade.

Morag had become older and bitter. She resented the power of the lairds and the quiet lives they led and decided that she must rule the land so she plotted against them.

She sat for many hours stroking the nose of Mournblade and thinking about their overthrow. Her biggest problem was the dragons. What to do about the dragons. There was no way she and Mournblade could conquer the land of the Scots with all those dragons.

Now, far away in the Highlands on a beach by the Loch of Neesh sat Mauw a dragon like no other. Mauw, pronounced Mao-ow, lay with his long tail and huge body in the water and his giant head resting on a rock. On his face was a contented smile. You see Mauw was special - he rarely stood on land and hardly ever flew preferring to swim in the cool cold waters of the deep loch. He was looked upon as wise and a leader by all the other dragons who, from time-to-time, flew down from the mountains to visit and talk of the good old days.

Meanwhile, on the Isle of Arran Morag the witch drew her plans. She gathered her army of trolls in front of her castle and climbed onto Mournblade's back.

"My pretties," she said. "My pretties, today will see the end of the dragons of the Scots. Today, we will put an end to the rule of the lairds. Today we shall rule the land of the Scots."

And with that an awful cheer rose from the ragged trolls and Mournblade hissed and shot a triumphant plume of fire into the sullen grey sky.

With one leap Mournblade rose into the sky with Morag screaming an old Campbell battle cry as her army marched forward waving their rusty claymores above their heads.

So loud and terrible was their cry that it could be heard many miles away.

Macleod, the dragon who guarded the land of Long Loch lay on his rock dreaming of flying above the clouds and awoke with a start. He lifted his head. He gazed into the distance. Something was wrong.

Straight away he flew into the air and gave the alarm, swooping low over the Castle of Duntrone and passing the message onto his brother dragons.

Inside the castles across the lands of the Scots the warlords and lairds gathered their armies and prepared themselves for battle. The dragons too prepared to safeguard their land and in the Loch of Neech Mauw took to the water and swam at speed down the Great Glen.

At the end of Loch Long stood the army of the wicked witch Morag, tattered banners fluttering in the breeze. At their head Mournblade, with Morag perched on her back, waited for battle to commence, an evil smile on their twisted lips.

On the horizon the great army of the Scots appeared, pipes playing, flags waving and cheering. Morag's army was pitifully small in comparison but Morag and Mournblade seemed somehow confident of victory.

And then silence covered the battlefield.

Suddenly the leaders of the Scots raised their swords and with a cry of "Alba Gabrach" - they moved forward. The flight of a dozen dragons launched themselves into the air and flew toward the evil trolls of Morag's army.

Mournblade took a hesitant step and shuffled ungainly forward to stand in the shallow waters of the loch. Morag raised her staff and spoke. And what she spoke poured fear into the army of the Scots. For it was a spell. Let me see if I can remember. It was:

"If dragon flying in air, If dragon on earth do sat,
Make dragon change to feline, Turn dragon into cat!"

High in the air the flight of dragons started to change. Their long tails became shorter, their heads became smaller, their scales and stripes became fur and with a horrified look on their faces they plummeted to the ground, no longer a dozen large and magnificent dragons, but small and frightened cats.

The Scots army stopped in its track and at that moment Mournblade took to the air. Morag raised her staff and bolts of lightening flew into the now retreating Scots army.

Everyone ran. They thought their time was up. I mean what can you do with a sword and a musket against a witch's magic?

Anyway Morag's soldiers moved forward and sensed victory.

But then from the dark Loch Neech came a rumble and the water boiled like an angry kettle. The ground shook and Mournblade and Morag turned and flew towards the loch. Hovering over it they looked down into the dark water trying to understand what it was.

Suddenly with a terrifying cry something shot upwards like a strange green streak of lightening from the water.

It was Mauw who had waited in silence for the right moment to strike. You see Morag's spell had changed all the dragons on land and in the air but she had forgotten about those of the water.

And as Mauw hurtled into the air he hissed in anger and fire belched from his mouth towards Mournblade, who flew towards the water in fright. But Mauw followed with the army of Scots cheering him on.

As he flew past he took a swipe at Mournblade with his talons and managed to scratch Mournblade's side who screeched in pain and anger. Morag held on to Mournblade's neck for dear life desperately trying to conjure up another spell and swatting the air with her staff.

Finally Mauw climbed high into the air and dived down to the tumbling Mournblade. Mauw hissed a final hiss and once again fire spat from his jaws and in one movement he hit Mournblade in the back with his tail. Mournblade fell to the ground into the centre of Morag's army. Lifeless and dead!

Morag's army was now running in terror. Morag, meanwhile, had managed to jump clear and fell with a tremendous splash into the cold waters of the Loch.

Mauw followed in pursuit and dived into the icy darkness grabbing Morag with his talons and after a terrifying scream Morag sank into the loch and was no more.

Mauw appeared some moments later with the witch's staff in his mouth which he broke in two with his jaws. He crawled onto the beach exhausted and cheered by the warlords, lairds and men of the army of the Scots.

On the beach to meet him was the small group of cats, who had once been the last dragons of Scotland.

They thanked him for saving their lives and agreed that in greeting their ancestors would ever honour his name. Mauw.

So, if you ever meet a stripy cat with thick fur and a huge M on its forehead who greets you with a "Mauw" then you're probably meeting one of the ancestors of the last dragons of Scotland.

And what happened to Mauw? I hear you ask.

Well the Loch of Neech where he lived is now known by the English name of Ness and folks do say that if you wait and watch long enough you'll maybe catch a glimpse of something playing in the dark waters of the loch. And if you do it's probably Mauw, the Last Dragon of Scotland.

Insufficient Evidence

Insufficient evidence to get a clean conviction
Insufficient evidence to prove a case at all
Subterfuge and undertones, attempted gross deception
Jealousy, possessiveness have caused this man to fall.

Insufficient evidence of bribery and corruption
Insufficient evidence of lying at the bar
Unjustified allusion to subversion and detection
Attempts at open warfare have pushed us both too far.

I've every right to silence your attempts at slur and slander
I've taken certain measures to stop this bitter war
You've pushed me to the edge of total confrontation
You've ignored negotiations and the why that talking's for
Chorus
Every appeal is a shot in the dark (Every plea is a bargain)
Every reply is with fury
Every court would let me go free
Every judge has a jury

I appeal to your heart I am innocent
I appeal to your heart I'm a free man
I appeal to your love to let me go free
I appeal to your love that you're guilty

Terminal Disease

"How can one define a computer virus? It is a software programme deliberately designed to introduce copies of itself into other programs, intent on causing relatively serious damage. Each infected program can then, in turn, infect other software. The behaviour and method of infection are similar to that of a virus of a living organism. That is where the analogy ends...."

An Introduction to Computer Viruses

Professor J. Arnold University of the West Midlands

Bristol, European Federal Republic, June 2038

Jon flicked down the pages of the day's copy of "Data Journal" eagerly scanning the jobs pages for a £350k a year, 25-hour a week, Project Leader position - a pitiful salary, he knew, but times were hard.

His current job was not unexciting - the job of Virus Co-ordinator was a responsible one and it certainly kept him and his hit squad on their toes. He had even been gifted with a nickname for his efforts - Doctor Kildare - a name alluding to a character from a 1960's soap opera currently being repeated. It was just that picking up the pieces from another unusable 786 or trying to refragment corrupt data blasted by yet another invasion of "Mobile 7" was beginning to wear very thin on frayed nerves.

Jon and his management regarded the job as integral to the business. He spent much of his getting to know his enemy - knowing their mode of attack. Being prepared. Kill or be killed. The poster behind his desk summed it up:

PREVENTION DETECTION ERADICATION

He was also committed to teaching basic procedures to prevent virus infection such as use of the standard detectors, taking back-ups as a reflex action, no input of external data without scanning.

He taught methods of spotting viruses such as longer boot up times, software performance problems, frequent errors, abnormal memory usage, corrupt or hidden files, all the basics.

OK. They didn't guarantee immunity but they would reduce contamination. But sometimes he felt that users just didn't realise the potential danger.

He thought back to the days when he was a young and spotty PC Programmer in the early 90's when Managers had been blinded by the sales patter of "cheap data processing" and "power to the users". They had fallen into the trap of distributed and uncontrollable insecure networks which could be broken into with the ease of a ten-year old with a few hours to kill during his half term hols or, more seriously, a highly-skilled prankster building sophisticated viruses attempting to outwit security.

What made viruses easier to infect was the ease of communications between what were originally stand-alone systems, but were now, with powerful netware, instantly accessible. Data was received to the "open systems" network by users from company partners and suppliers via EDI, NET*POST and other mailing systems with no other protection than the continually out-of-date Anti Virus filter software with a mission to seek and destroy incoming viruses prior to network infection but, due to the mutability of many viruses it was exceedingly ineffective.

In the late 90's the installation of a games disk became a sack able offence and this had considerably reduced the risks of infection and the restriction had been extended to any unapproved product or software even if scanned by all filters prior to installation. Cyber terrorism was the last straw but even the so called impenetrable firewalls had holes.

What was making the battle harder was the access to PCs which every household had. Neighbours, friends and family could cyber chat cheaply across home LANs. Software was cheap, available and easily copied (even though this did breach every copyright law in the book). Games computers allowed buddies to play each other remotely at games such as "WIPEOUT V37" (in which it was perfectly acceptable to hack into an opponent's software to cheat and fix a game).

Each new game pushed games firms to be the highest grossing world-wide corporations with a monthly profit higher than Brazil's national debt.

The revelation that one computer giant had actively encouraged viruses in order to sell more PCs to replace burnt-out ones and to sell (useless) anti-virus software had been a worrying aspect.

There had been a public outcry, of course, and the Managing Director had resigned, but it was obvious that through the shallow denials the competition was doing the same.

In one renowned infection a bank, who had rushed a little too headlong into the new technological networking craze, had been brought to its knees by a computer science student who had hacked into the bank's network, aiming to alter his and his colleague's bank accounts to increase balances. His hacking had been not completely successful. In fact every one of the bank's accounts had been corrupted. A day's transactions were lost which caused a total lack of confidence in the bank. The electronic closure of accounts by its customers via home-banking systems affected a run on the bank and within days it went into liquidation, eventually being bailed out by the European Bank of Commerce.

By the late 90's viruses had reached epidemic proportions - no longer confined to the detectable such as Michelangelo, Danube and Jerusalem - the new generation of "perverted" software was uncontrollable and most agreed contamination of a PC was inevitable even with strict preventative measures. Something radical was called for.

The 1998 Electronic Vandalism Act which had made the distribution and authorship of viruses an offence carried a fine and a sentence of up to five years imprisonment. However, the police, with a reduced budget and resource, found it difficult to trace, yet alone convict the vandals. Few were caught, authorship was difficult to prove and they were always clever enough to cover their tracks.

One conservative estimate for 2007 put the number of undetected new viruses infecting global networks to be 57 per day - dependent on university and school holidays.

Newer hardware development which extended the idea of diskless work stations prevalent in the mid-90's to processor-less work stations meant all software was only stored and accessible in one server. This made tracking down viruses even easier since they could only reside in limited areas.

Perhaps there would be further improvements with the installation in the near future of the central processor/disks and processor/diskless work stations - the modern Server Mainframe approach - but only time would tell.

The telephone rang, waking him from his day dream.

"Hello," he said, "Virus Co-ordination?"

"My name's Pete Moseley, Information Research, 1st Floor", the voice replied agitatedly, "I've got a message on my screen, it says, 'PC Infected by Virus - Call Your Co-ordinator', can you help??"

"OK", Jon said scrabbling for his Anti-Virus Kit, "I'll be right down."

The kit was a simple device containing his 'little Sherlock' and a micro monitor which could be plugged into any PC port to perform various diagnostic traces. It was a highly useful tool which rarely let him down. His only other tools were instinct and experience - a nose for sniffing out vermin.

He slammed the security door and hurried down the corridor towards the stairs up to the second floor. In Information Research, he shook hands with the user (a mandatory greeting, the product of German management practises). Pete got up and turned his monitor around exposing the windowed message on the screen, invoked by the background virus protection software which randomly checked original versions of software installed and those executed. It had done its job. It had found a difference and had reported it.

"Look," Moseley said obviously wanting to leave, "I'll just pop to the top floor, couple of people I want to see," and he left Jon on his own.

Jon set about unpacking his kit. He cleared the message icon by rebooting the processor. He immediately checked the primary, secondary and tertiary drives for obvious virus intrusion, but as expected, found no trace in the likely directories.

He would have to be careful in case the virus had a protection mechanism which erased memory, storage and then itself, disappearing, as if by magic, up its own entry point!

He ran the standard virus searches and drew a blank. He was about to give in when he applied his own virus checker built from years of painful infection eradication - this showed a 'Trojan horse' corrupting the operating system.

It was running in the background which usually indicated it was replicating itself and sending reproductions primarily to any external address it could find as it scanned "electronic mailing" software for nicknames, internal mailboxes and remote locations.

Most viruses detected were 'pranksters' or 'teasers' that flashed up logos and messages which were more of an annoyance than a threat, some were 'falses' which corrupted the odd file and deleted memory.

This virus was obviously the worst and most serious type, a 'killer'. 'Killers' were self-replicating viruses which spread like a brushfire and were out to inflict maximum damage by corrupting memory, deleting back-ups and erasing software. 'Killers' were sometimes written by disgruntled ex-employees bearing a grudge, sometimes by unscrupulous competitors aiming to destroy a company's info-base and credibility and sometimes by politically-motivated groups.

Jon immediately isolated the machine and removed all the cables from outputs and ports - probably a futile exercise since it would have been reproducing itself exponentially since detection.

He captured a copy of the virus and filtered it through his own hardware which did an electronic autopsy on the module - analysing it to decode origin, age, source, author, name, in fact anything which might identify the protagonist or help its eradication.

He found a module name - "GUILLAME" and a description name imbedded in the load module - "GUILLAME BARRE". Author's name was shown as "Militant Dawn" - whoever they were? It struck him that finding this information had been far too easy - source data was being handed to him on a plate, no pretence had been made to hide it.

Anyway, after he had found a method of deletion he would call it all into the Virus Control Centre in London and they could begin writing protection and detection software. With luck it would be down the wire within four hours.

So. Deletion? He would try the easiest method first. He entered the command: *Erase GUILLAME*

And waited for a response...

Suddenly the screen filled with a swirling spiralling fractal pattern. The mesmerizing patterns seemed to make his face glow with a strange warmth. At the centre of the pattern a dot began to grow in size, filling up the entire screen like a black hole opening up before him.

"WELCOME TO THE GUILLAME BARRE VIRUS", it said

"YOUR POOR ATTEMPT AT DELETION HAS INVOKED THE PROTECTION MECHANISM!"

"UNTIL NOW COMPUTER VIRUSES WERE ISOLATED TO HARDWARE AND SOFTWARE AND WERE NOT OF AN ORGANIC NATURE".

"UNTIL NOW...."

"THE AUTHORS OF GUILLAME BARRE ARE PROUD TO ANNOUNCE THE FIRST ELECTRONICALLY TRANSMITTED, GENETICALLY ENGINEERED, ORGANIC VIRUS".

"IT WAS WRITTEN TO SOUND THE DEATH KNELL OF THE CAPITALIST STATE."

"IT WAS WRITTEN BY THE ONES WHO WAIT."

"IT WAS WRITTEN AS AN ACT OF TERRORISM."

"THE VIRUS YOU AND YOUR ORGANISATION HAVE JUST CONTRACTED IS A GENETICALLY ENGINEERED STRAIN OF NERVE FLU GENERATED VIA FRACTAL IMAGES AND TRANSMITTED VIA THE ELECTROMAGNETIC STATIC EMISSIONS FROM YOUR TERMINAL."

"THE VIRUS ATTACKS NERVE ENDINGS. FIRST SYMPTOMS ARE A TINGLING SENSATION IN THE FINGER TIPS."

"IT IS HIGHLY VIRULENT. IT IS HIGHLY INFECTIOUS."

"THERE IS NO CURE. THERE IS NO ANTIDOTE."

Jon was frozen in fear. Petrified. He moved forward to try to hit the POWER OFF button but his muscles seemed to have no power and his body no will to move. His fingers and toes tingled with pins and needles. He felt stiff. He felt nauseous, numb, a dull warmth coursing throughout his body. His breath was becoming tight and difficult.

"BY THE TIME YOU HAVE COMPLETED THIS, YOUR INTRODUCTION TO OUR MOVEMENT, YOUR ORGANISATION'S NETWORK WILL BE PARALYSED AND YOU WILL BE A VICTIM OF ITS GREED, IGNORANCE AND INDIFFERENCE."

The virus worked quickly closing down the vital parts of his body. The room began to fade. His body slumped from the chair on the ground.

Around the building he could hear shouts and screams and the sound of panic. He closed his eyes and prostrate on the floor, fighting for breath, he blacked out. His heart stopped.

His pager went off.

Give Me Back My Heart

I've never believed in angels or heaven and love without end
I've never conceived of a sorrow when the words weren't already penned
But I held you that evening by moonshine, when the night was bright as the day
And now I have nothing of value, now my heart's been stolen away

Chorus

Give me back my heart!	You took it, you ripped me apart
Give me back my heart!	You took it, please give it back
Give me back my heart!	You took it, you threw it away
Give me back my heart!	You took it, I trusted your feelings

For now I have nothing of value now my heart's been stolen away...

I trusted you with my possessions, all that I had would be yours
And I never revealed where the key was, kept it locked-up inside behind doors
But you found it and started this aching that haunts me by night and by day
And you left me with nothing of value now my heart's been stolen away

Chorus

There's nothing more that I can give you, just my love and my hopes and my fears
But my love and my hopes are in tatters and my smiles have been turned into tears
If only I could find what you've taken, on that night as bright as day
Just barren with nothing of value now my heart's been stolen away

Chorus

The Man Who Never Was

"Oh what a tangled web we weave!
Oh how one little lie leads to a much bigger one!"

A sea of desks as far as the eye can see, the modern office, about as impersonal as one could get. Years hence and their cramped spacing would have described them as inhumane but in Barmids Bank this was the norm. Space a very premium and charged by the square metre back to the cost centre. This Monday morning the space police were out in force. With a raft of new starters a spare desk would be filled and charged back to a cost centre quicker than a Labrador on leftovers.

In the IT department the office layout, to allow furrowed brows to be further furrowed, was in groups of four. A grim brown hessian screen separated the teams giving some autonomy and privacy. Even so, space was at the time highly priced and a desk rarely stayed empty for long. Each gang of four guarded its area robustly and any excess space was swelled weekly with a fresh intake of clean-faced students who thought the Battle of Britain was fought at Hastings in 1066 and that irony was only slightly stronger than bronzy.

On this Monday, Martin, Pete and Jon were answering their first emails and contemplated the empty desk in front of them. The previous Friday, after a very long and expensive lunch one of their number had departed to pastures new and their desk was now vacant. And then there were three.

As the day wore on they knew that at some point the space police would arrive and a someone called Kevin with spots, halitosis and a degree in Media Studies from West Midlands University would be assigned to them. For the two or three hours they had with the empty space they spread out and the empty desk was used for various activities, mini meetings, laying out manuals, the lunch-time card school and collating reports.

Then that fateful hour arrived. Reg, the office services manager, chief inspector of free space was on the prowl.

He cruised the offices like a basking shark looking for weak and easy prey. The glare of a clean worktop attracted him like the Lord to a leper.

Then his keen piercing eyes spotted it. Desk! Empty? At three o'clock. In for the kill! Attack! Attack! Attack! He crossed the office and arrived at the pod. The gang of three look up sensing defeat.

"Excuse me," Reg said, eyes twinkling, "is this desk empty?"

Peter looked at Jon, Jon looked at Martin, Martin looked at Peter desperately playing for a few additional seconds. They had to think quickly. Suddenly Martin took up the challenge, "No!" he said lying through his teeth, "Er. It isn't!" he continued hesitantly.

Reg sniffed the air. Could he smell a rat? Was that the odour of the bullshit spray he had detected? "Well. It certainly looks vacant," Reg said suspiciously. "Who occupies it?" he asked, interrogating them further.

Martin for a moment looked stumped. They looked at each other again with hope, desperately trying to prompt Martin or give him some inspiration. "Improvise! Improvise! Improvise!" Peter and Jon both willed him.

In a moment of inspiration Martin snatched the answer from the ether, "Oh!" he said confidently, "Mike Williams sits there."

Reg narrowed his eyes in a combination of surprise and disappointment. He was still not totally convinced. He had been caught before. In 1977. With the out-to-lunch incident. "So where is he then?" he probed.

"Oh errrr," Martin flustered, "he's got a day off. He'll be back tomorrow."

Reg grunted and with a look that bore a very close resemblance to an Arnie "I'll be back" he clutched tightly to his clipboard and departed to patrol other more fruitful waters.

The gang of three sighed in relief. Then slowly their situation and predicament dawned on them. Like Frankenstein they had spawned a monster. Mike Williams had been born. How were they to perpetuate the tangled web of deceit that had been woven?

Immediately, they drew up their plans. They plotted. They conspired. Their first task was to set up the Mike Williams monitor.

A schedule was drawn up and every week it was the task of a different member of the team to ensure that Mike's desk and work area, when not in use for other activities, looked lived in and occupied.

Jon brought in an old suit jacket and anorak from home. The jacket was placed on the back of the chair and the coat hung on a hanger on the partition next to the desk. During the day this gave the appearance of occupancy and at night both were folded in the empty drawer. They decorated the partitions around the desk with the usual paraphernalia such as "You Want It When?" pictures, process diagrams, telephone lists, a calendar (with various dates highlighted), a poster of U2 and some old postcards.

Daily, the "Mike Williams Monitor" placed reports and manuals open on the desk, with highlighter pens, biros and pencils laid out to give the appearance of work in progress.

A bright red china mug and an old stained drinks coaster were brought in. The mug was occasionally filled with hot coffee. Mike's angle-poise light was connected to a time switch under the desk so it magically came on first thing in the morning and last thing at night. The phone was still connected for their former colleague and they had it registered under Mike's name so he appeared in the internal and on-line telephone directory.

They began sending Mike internal mail and then decided to subscribe Mike to free magazines. His job title was "Disk Driver." The existence of Mike on a mailing list spawned lots of "junk" mail and soon Mike started receiving a regular and healthy post by snail- and email. At Christmas and even on Valentine's Day Mike was never forgotten. On his birthday they bought the whole section doughnuts.

With a stroke of genius they gave Mike a family by buying a cheap Supasnap photo frame with one of those glossy generic family photos in it. This was placed strategically on Mike's desk. Mike became a married man with two glowing children. Now Mike had a character. Each of them had a mental picture what he was like and could anticipate what Mike would do in certain situations such as whether he fancied a cup of coffee or to go home early on a Friday. They knew the music, books and TV programmes he liked or disliked. They made him a Wolves supporter. Well someone had to.

Mike's fame began to spread. They provided a system for Mike to support with a few programmes that hardly ever ran. The Dummy Inventory System ran on request, had no input and no output.

For various reasons Mike started to receive phone calls and staff looking for him, so stock excuses were invented and applied to explain his absence such as "he's away talking to the user," "he's just nipped off to the loo," "he's gone to sort out a system problem," "he's visiting our other site," “he’s taken a day off” or “he’s on a course”.

After a while Mike became quite a chore and adjoining partitions were let into the secret to participate in the pretence, helping to further perpetuate Mike's existence. Christmas, New Year and Easter gave times of some relaxation when they awarded Mike extra long holidays. And he never forgot to send the team a post card.

But one day the inevitable happened; Mike's non-existence was discovered. The system next on the list to the Dummy Inventory System had crashed and Mike's name had been accidentally picked for call-out and support but of course was unobtainable. His home number was in fact a Pizza Take-Away hot-line.

The trail of intensive management enquiry led to the group of desks and they were very politely pulled over the coals by the boss. So they decided that Mike's contract should be terminated and so sadly, within days, Mike left the company. He was removed from mailing and distribution lists. His jacket was put away and his desk was cleared for good.

In memoriam a collection and card were organised and funds were put towards a leaving party. His leaving party was one of the best that had ever been held and a seat was kept for Mike throughout the evening. They even decided that a strip-o-gram would have not only been inappropriate but would also have been a very one-sided affair. The evening was spent in beery contemplation. It was what Mike would have wanted. They were really going to miss him and it was decreed by the team that henceforth his birthday, the day they saved the desk, should be celebrated in future years.

Not long after, Reg, on one his regular trawls, spotted and filled Mike's old desk with a new starter. The day the new colleague started, the mail man arrived delivering his usual bundle. He spotted the new starter and after introducing himself said, "Ah, and you must be Mike Williams! Good to meet you at long last! How's the family?"

Shot in the Dark

Nowhere to run, nowhere to hide
Nowhere to seek, nowhere to find,
Nowhere to go, nowhere to cry,
Nowhere, no one, no way, no why.

'Cos you're a runner on a laserjet.
A fast loose mover a winner but yet
You're a lover on an ebbing tide
A loser with nowhere to run, nowhere to hide.

Nothing to hold, nothing to see
Nothing to want, no one to be
Never alone always on fire
Wanting to rest, can't stop til you get higher.

Shot in the dark, I'm right on target
Stabbed in the back from the others behind
Flash in the pan famed for fifteen
Minutes to run. Cheating you blind.
Fired the bullet straight on target.
Turn the spark to a flame, all in the mind

Angels

They are all around;
In the air, in the trees, in the towns
Even in the architecture
You may find a tiny white feather
You may find a sudden sweet fragrance under your nose
You may see a bright light or colour in the mind's eye
You may feel a tingling in the air
You may feel their loving warmth

For the archangels guide them;
Gabriel for hope, joy, dreams and communication
Chamael for courage, empowerment and justice
Michael for strength, protection, truth, fighting for right
Zadkiel for abundance, wisdom, success and justice
Haniel for love, compassion and beauty
Cassiel for peace, harmony and serenity
Raphael for healing, energy and knowledge

We are each other's angels, we meet when it is time.
I've seen and met angels,
Wearing the disguise of ordinary people
People living ordinary lives.

The difference between a person and an angel is easy.
Most of an angel is in the inside
Most of a person is on the outside.

We are all born as angels
Only as our legs increase in size so our wings decrease.
But for every blade of grass, every sunflower,
Every tree, every bluebell, every oak is an angel
Saying grow, bloom, blossom, grow. Be!

One day, we shall hear the angels
One day, we shall see their wings open
One day, we shall see the sky sparkling with diamonds.
One day, we shall find peace.

Alpha to Omega

A night like any other
Before the days of old
Chose the lady darkness
Darkness over love and gold
Every day the battle
Fight the first and last
Given to the leaders
Hatred of future past
Intolerable and wasted
Justice was not the best
Knights were killed in action
Lost amongst the rest
Mighty were the angels
Never fainting tears
Open were the masters
Purged of all their fears
Quick the dead were taken
Rushed toward the light
Saved were all the righteous
Taken before the night
Under clouds of thunder
Vain and lost were gone
Weakened by the wonder
Xeno-morphed the one
Youth prayed to graven image
Zero shall overcome.

Last Man Standing

"..or how the belief in invincibility can be shattered with disastrous consequences."

The legend of what happened on a scorching day in June 1876 when hundreds of Indian warriors converged on a ridge above the Little Big Horn River has been contributed to by historians, artists and movie producers. The image of Custer standing alone on a grassy hillock dressed in buckskins, pistols blazing at circling Indians, his fallen comrades at his feet, is the picture that has been painted. Over a century later many questions remain unanswered.

At the end of the American Civil War Major General George Armstrong Custer was, at 25, a national hero with thoughts of a Presidential bid. His next command was as Lieutenant Colonel to the 7th Cavalry with whom he led campaigns against the northern Indians. Treaties were signed and broken, land taken and the Indians forced from one inhospitable reservation to another. Teton Chief Red Cloud said "The white man made only one promise that they kept. They said they would take our land and they took it."

In December 1875 the Indians attacked prospectors in the Black Hills who had invaded the reservations. In response the government ordered Sioux and Cheyenne to report to the Indian agencies by January 1876 or be branded hostile. The deadline and ultimatum were received with disdain. It was what the government hoped for and the army were dispatched to force the Indians out. With news spreading of war the Indians began to gather in larger numbers and alliances were made against the common enemy.

By June 1876 the Indians were camped on the Rosebud River where they had paused for the ceremony of the sun dance. After this intense experience Sitting Bull had a prophetic vision of seeing dead soldiers "falling right into our camp".

When army scouts located the village a plan was devised to prevent the Indians' escape, most believing that if attacked the Indians would scatter.

However, with the Indians united in a determination to fight against those who would seize the Black Hills their resolve was further hardened by Sitting Bull's vision.

On June 22nd Custer left Fort Lincoln with his command of officers, enlisted men, Indian scouts and guides totalling 645. His two senior subordinates were Major Reno and Captain Benteen and the column included three of Custer's relatives including his brother, brother-in-law and nephew who was on a summer's outing with his uncle.

Meanwhile, the Indian village's size had swelled from 800 to 2,500 warriors and was located on the Little Bighorn with tepees sprawled along the river for nearly two miles, largely hidden by trees and protected to the east by ragged bluffs.

On June 24th Custer correctly surmised that the Indians were now on the Little Bighorn River and immediately ordered a night march to within 15 miles of the village. As June 25th dawned Custer's scouts spotted smoke rising to the west. Worried that the Indians would detect his column and flee, Custer decided to attack the village as soon as possible. At noon the column was divided into three battalions. Reno commanded one group to attack the village from the south-east, Benteen commanded another to stop any Indians escaping south, while Custer retained 225 men to ride along the ridge and attack from the north.

Riding his men towards the camp Reno flushed out a handful of Sioux warriors and followed them. Ironically he came close to surprising the Indians, who had only minutes before the soldiers struck and some 200 warriors rode out to face the soldiers. As the Indians approached Reno ordered his men to dismount to fight on foot and the advance immediately ground to a halt as more Indians joined the fray.

Under fierce attack Reno abandoned his position and ordered his men to remount. His battalion was in disarray and his orders were either not heard or confused. Seized by panic, the remnants now scurried up the ravine and onto the bluffs.

To the north of the village out of sight of Reno's predicament Custer had halted his column. Worried about ammunition he sent a courier to Benteen.

His last message said "Benteen. Come on. Big Village. Be Quick. Bring packs. P.Bring pacs." The final misspelled words showing the haste that it had been written.

Spurring his horse on the courier glanced over his shoulder to see Custer leading his men down into a ravine that led to the village. Here Custer was met with stiff resistance from warriors who had broken off the fight with Reno and had hurried to meet the attackers. Many of his men dismounted, while others retreated back up the ravine to higher ground.

Finally, what remained of Custer's command gathered in three groups along the ridge laying down volleys to keep the Indians at bay. The Indians made few charges but kept up long-range fire from behind sage-brush and the long grass while arrows fell with deadly effect on clusters of exposed troops which took a heavy toll

Although each of the three groups made its "last stand" the one of legend occurred on the northern end of the ridge. After a final counter attack, the survivors gathered around Custer's banner shooting their horses for breastworks as they were attacked from all sides by warriors including the legendary Crazy Horse. The Indians, defending homes and families, full of a sense of power and injustice, did their work thoroughly and the battle was over within an hour. Custer and his command were wiped out.

Benteen, further up the trail, was met by Custer's courier. Arriving in the valley Benteen saw the last of Reno's men retreating into the bluffs. A short gallop and Benteen met up with a panicked Reno, "For God's sake, Benteen, halt your command and help me. I've lost half my men." To the north they could hear the sound of gunfire but neither Reno nor Benteen made any move to rush to the sounds as required by the orders the courier had bought.

Soon warriors began to return to the bluff to continue the onslaught and it was pounded until darkness fell. In the village the soldiers could hear the sounds of celebration. Next morning the Indians poured arrows and bullets into the defences of the bluff. Counter attacks were mounted to push back the attackers until in the afternoon the firing subsided. Early in the evening the Indians torched the prairie grass creating smoke to screen the village and a great procession emerged from behind the smoke. Sitting Bull had ordered the Indians to break camp believing that there would be retribution for their victory over "Yellow Hair".

The next day General Terry's column arrived. His scouts had already discovered the answer to Reno's first question. Where was Custer? On the ridge they had counted over 200 bodies littering the ground. Most had been stripped, scalped and mutilated. Custer had been stripped but neither scalped nor mutilated and had been killed by a bullet to his left breast and his left temple. The only survivor, contrary to legend, was an officer's horse called Comanche. The dead were hastily buried in shallow graves and marked with small wooden posts.

When the news of Custer's annihilation reached Washington it was a day after the July 4th centennial celebration and President Grant's first reaction was disbelief. When announced to the country the news brought the wrath of a nation down on all Indians that ended only with the massacre of Wounded Knee in 1890.

Questions still reverberate about why the defeat happened. Was it Custer's thirst for glory to strengthen his hope for a Presidential nomination? Reno's ineffective command? Benteen's inaction? To allocate blame is to do the Indians a disservice - the Army lost because the Indians won.

Today the battlefield is a National Monument. It is an intensely moving place - white marble headstones trail up from the ravine and mark the retreat of Custer's command. In the central cluster of men on the hill top is Custer's stone, the legendary last man standing.

I Have Learnt

16th March 2008
Aged 50

I have learnt….
There is a choice we have between;
hate and hurt and ignorance and derision and jealousy and
envy and evil and wickedness and rob and grasp and greed and
avarice and lies and perjury and propaganda and falsehoods and
half truths and dishonesty and distrust and
weasel words and twist and spin and bribery and corruption and
pain and grief and sorrow and anger and agony and torture and
abhorrence and detestation and revenge and retribution and
subdue and crush and defeat and extinguish and crush and
reprisal and revulsion and disgust and pity and
fear and loathing and dislike and distaste and
damage and break and spoil and trash and wreck and ruin and
destroy and destruction and mutilate and wipe out and
terminate and war and conflict and combat and confrontation and
battle and struggle and jihad and crusade and
feud and fight and slay and destroy and
destruction and extermination and genocide and murder and
kill and obliterate and annihilate and demolish and devastate and
all things which darken our world.

And the choice is L O V E.

Broken Promises

"They made us many promises, more than I can remember, but they never kept but one;

They promised to take our land, and they took it."

It began with Columbus in October 1492 who, landing at San Salvador at the settlement of Tainos, gave them the name Indios. As was the custom with visitors the Tainos on the island of San Salvador gave them gifts and treated them with honour. All this was taken as some sign of weakness and the Spanish in return promised that those in the New World would "adopt our ways".

Over the next four hundred years several million Europeans and their descendants undertook to enforce their ways on the people of the New World.

The Europeans who followed Columbus destroyed the New World's vegetation and its inhabitants - human, animal, bird, fish and minerals after turning it into a wasteland. Then they abandoned it.

Red Cloud, Chief of the Tetons said, "They made us many promises, more than I can remember, but they never kept but one; they promised to take our land, and they took it."

Four hundred years later in 1890 when the last remnants of the great tribes were finally slaughtered at Wounded Knee no one chose to ask:

But, where are the Pequot, the Wampanoags, the Miamis? Where are the Narraganseet, the Sauks, the Pokanet? Where are the Winnebagos, the Pottawotamies and the Kickapoos ? What is left of the Sioux, the Cheyenne, the Apache, the Arapaho, the Comanche, the Navajo, the Cherokee, the Choctaws, the Creeks, the Seminoles? Of the Sante, Shawnee, Ottawa, Hurons, Delaware, Modocs, Mohaves, Paiutes, Shastas and Yumas?

Only Pocohantas of the Powhatan and Uncas of the Mohican are remembered.

And where now are the people Columbus called the Indios? Where now are the Tainos?

Their last breath was four hundred years later at a place called Wounded Knee.

Some ten years after the Battle of the Little Bighorn when the plains people had been hunted to extinction a few hundred were camped in the deep snow in a field at a place called Wounded Knee. After a misunderstanding trying to disarm a deaf Indian warrior the US Cavalry opened fire and slaughtered 350 men women and children.

It was on the fourth day after Christmas 1890 and the handful of survivors sheltered in an Episcopal mission hall close to the field.

As the torn and bleeding bodies of the wounded were carried into the candlelit church which was decked with Christmas greenery in the rafters, a soldier noticed the crudely lettered banner stretched across the chancel above the pulpit.

It said:

"Peace on Earth, Good Will to All Men"

Adapted from Bury my Heart at Wounded Knee
by
Dee Brown

I Wish

I wish for a church without ignorance, only understanding

I wish for it to have no cathedral, for God and his love is all around

I wish for a religion in which all are as one

I wish for it to have no boundaries or barriers from nations for beliefs

I wish for it to have no leaders only followers

I wish for it to teach love for all and by example

I wish it to know there is hope and innocence in the world

I wish for it to serve without thought for reward

I wish it to enrich all regardless of race, religion, colour or creed.

I wish it to heal neighbours, community and planet

I wish it to know the whole planet as a being and part of ourselves.

I wish it to see the great idea without prejudice and envy.

I wish it to have no fear or shame or hate or anger.

I wish it to do these things without hope of reward now or in the hereafter except the joy of doing it.

I wish its followers to be known not by a badge or a book but by a smile and the God in their eyes.

I wish it not to preach but be seen by its actions

I wish it to honour all those who have gone before.

I wish these things so that the world will change

only if we change ourselves.

I wish it to understand and know the supremacy of love.

And that all shall belong.

Piers

For my brother. Larger than life,
I miss his warmth and laughter
I envied his total disregard for convention.
God bless and keep him!

As some of you may know I write a few stories in my spare time. When I thought of my brother Piers I thought about the great stories he will leave behind. Some of them are just wonderful. Beyond fiction. Some of them are unbelievable.

The earliest was as a teenager. He was showing off tightrope walking on the huge gas pipes being laid behind my Granny's home in Dorset. I left him at it and went off doing my own thing. Some hours later I found him lying on the sofa with his leg in plaster. Apparently he had come up with a particularly clever manoeuvre and while frantically shouting and waving at me he had slipped and fallen 15 feet into the trench under the pipes.

Some years later Piers and I had been given the perennial task of clearing out the garage. The day was damp and wet. As most of the rubbish had been burnable he had loaded an old metal bin with wooden staves so it now resembled a large jar of cocktails sticks. Of course lighting it became impossible. So Piers had come up with the idea of drenching it with a couple of gallons of petrol, which he poured copiously over the wood. He then took a burning torch of paper and gingerly lit it. At which point, standing ten yards away behind a wall, I saw him disappear momentarily in a large fireball and explosion of black smoke. He reappeared with a blackened and somewhat surprised face minus eyebrows and some of his hair. He said, "Mmmm… we need more kindling…"

You see, you can't write stuff like that!

Piers then took to cars and after passing his test he bought a very old and battered Austin A60, which he freely admitted needed attention. We would quibble on what attention it needed.

I would have advocated a complete overhaul, bodywork, shocks, exhaust, engine, clutch you name it.

For Piers attention meant:

1. Fitting a very powerful car stereo with speakers everywhere

2. Lay carpets for passenger and driver

3. Fit a very small steering wheel the size of a Polo mint so that by tweaking it a millimetre the vehicle would turn 180 degrees, and

4. A coat of paint in bright sunshine yellow.

Seeing me about to walk the short distance to my girlfriend's he said, "Want a lift?" Without thinking I said, "Yes..." We set off at break-neck speed heading at 80mph towards the bottom of the road. I pointed out that the lamp post was metal. He said "Ah yes, but the fence is wooden." By pumping the brakes we managed to slow down enough to take the corner safely.

Relaxing now he switched on the radio and the rock sounds of ELP belted at 98Db from everywhere including under my seat. As I investigated this feat of sound technology – he had taken an old set of 40W speakers and wedged them in the rear passengers' foot well - I lifted the carpet and saw through a hole approximately a foot square (in metric that's bloody big) and to my utter panic and delight the road whizzing past below me. I put the carpet back as it offered some small protection. At least I couldn't see it. As we went by pedestrians, cyclists and other road users waved to us gaily. Or at least that's what I think they did. Arriving at my girlfriend's, which thankfully was at the top of a hill and which required little brake pumping, we graunched and squeaked to a halt with the sound of four large iron disks being ground against rough concrete.

I ejected from the vehicle by climbing through the window (the door handle was missing) and he turned the car 180 degrees (he couldn't get reverse) and roared back down the hill in a cloud of dark acrid smoke leaving my future parents-in-law and their neighbours aghast. Was it a bird? Was it a plane? Nope it was my big brother.

Later Piers picked me up. My girlfriend told me she knew we had arrived home as ten minutes later the distant sound ceased abruptly.

Having had limited success with own my wall building – many described it as "pretty hopeless really" - Piers volunteered to help with some building work in bricking up a garage. Without aid of spirit level, tape or plumb line which would have hindered the process, the seven-foot wall began to rise. At the third course it developed a slight buckle. Not to worry he said, "We'll correct it on the next..." and so the wall took shape with Piers throwing up bricks on the construction and making course corrections as we went. By the final brick the wall now looked like a melting chocolate bar. The plan was that once the wall was dry we could correct its rakish quality with copious layers of cement until no one would be any the wiser. With the final brick laid Piers shouted a triumphant "....finished!" from behind the wall. Seconds later he reappeared as the wall collapsed in a pile of breezeblocks and wet cement at our feet. "Bugger!" he said.

Some years later Piers was staying with me when I organised a BBQ for my friends and colleagues in our back garden - nothing more than a very large field. With the sun sinking Piers wandered off to the bottom of the garden for a cigarette and with his hands in his pockets he admired the view. One of my colleagues walked out on the patio and said, "....nice place Mark, but why the scarecrow?" "Scarecrow?" I said. "Yes, scarecrow" she replied and pointed down the meadow at Piers. "That's not a scarecrow!" I said "...that's my Big Brother", at which moment Piers turned and waved causeing my friend to almost jump out of her skin in fright and drop her drink.

Then there was the time when in an effort to save a few bob he decided to take on the task of moving the extremely large eight-berth trailer caravan. Attaching this large monolith to the back of his Triumph Dolomite and with its boot and exhaust dragging on the floor he set off at high speed around the Welsh lanes. What he'd forgotten was the caravan's tiny wheels were only designed for very short and slow distances and not for a 60-mile drag at light speed behind a straining Dolomite.

Predictably, but much to Piers' surprise, the tyres blew leaving him and his load stranded. Picture if you would the face of the AA Relay driver as he arrived in the middle of nowhere to face the recovery of a very large caravan, blocking a very narrow Welsh lane.

What was left of its tiny wheel rims was still red hot with a chap standing with arms folded by a smoking and battered Triumph Dolomite and being greeted by the words, "Well! You took your bloody time..."

My final Piers story concerns his last words. I told him that I loved him. He was my big brother after all. His reply was typically Piers. You'll have to excuse my language but it was something that meant "Oh! Go Forth and Multiply, You Person of Very Doubtful Parentage".

Those of you who knew Piers will not find this at all surprising. Indeed thinking about it this was exactly how he often greeted his brothers, including of course David, if they came into his room for any reason whatsoever. It would not surprise me if in those last moments, he had recognised a brother come to greet him and that's why he said what he said and why he went so swiftly.

Whatever the reason, if God needs the garage tidying or a wall building or a car repairing he could do a lot worse than go to Piers. He could do a lot better of course but I know God likes a good laugh.

Meanwhile, I know everyone of my family has similar tales to tell.

Thankfully, Piers and all those great stories will always be with us.

God Bless and Keep Him.

I Wanna...

I have seen the wars and all the pain
I have seen the storms and all the rain
I have lost my faith in hollow dreams
I have lost my hope and what it means
I have known the politicians lie
I have known the faithless fail and die
I have seen the armies break their swords
I have heard the lies behind the words.

Chorus

I wanna know, the reason for the rhyme
I wanna know, the truth behind the crime
I wanna see, the want of all these years
I wanna see, the end of all these tears
I wanna know, that all is not yet lost
I wanna know, that the fight is worth the cost
I wanna see, that hope will win the day
I wanna see, that love's the only way

I have seen that humans lost the race
I have seen the weak can't stand the pace
I have lost the will to fight the tide
I have lost the strength to be a guide
I have known the need to stay or go
I have known the sound of yes and no
I have seen my enemies cut and run
I have heard my friends put down the gun.

I have seen and watched the bridges burn
I have seen the earth stop in its turn
I have lost if I throw it all away
I have lost if I do not face the day
I have known it's best to stand your ground
I have known that love will surely be found
I have seen the change from wrong to right
I have seen the candle illuminate the night

Who?

Who shall find the grail
Who shall find the one
Who shall find the perfect
Who shall find the sun
Who shall break the silence
Who shall break the night
Who shall break the barriers
Who shall break the light
Who shall open windows
Who shall open minds
Who shall open peace talks
Who shall open hands
And when we find the answer
And when we find the peace
And when it's time for laughter
Will war and suffering cease?

It's Your Song

I want to see the silent sabotage,
I want to see the sand of time,
I want to hear the silent enemy,
I want to taste the sweetness of the wine.

Oh, how I miss you. Oh, how I long.
Oh, just to kiss you. Oh, here's your song.

I want to stop the open hostility,
I want to have the upper hand,
I want to end all the insanity,
I want to hold love in my hand.

Oh, how I hold you. Oh, how I belong.
Oh, how I kiss you. Oh, this is your song.

I want to cease the senseless suffering,
I want to end the war and pain,
I want to show love's a certainty,
I want to dry the tears and rain.

The Reason Why

Saw myself in the the mirror the other day
Saw myself in the looking glass another way
Am just another lonely man walking the street
Or do I need to start feeling that lonely heart beat
Could I try to find a way to run and hide
Was it easier to fight than to turn the tide
Was it harder trying to walk the line
Maybe I should try to give just a little more time

You can run but you cant hide, You can swim but the rivers wide
You can jump but you can't fly, You should ask the reason why...

Saw my reflection in my fellow man
Saw the way I should be not the way I am
Pushing harder than I really should
Being louder than I ever could
Have to find a way of being cool
Have to work even harder to play be the rules
Have to make the world better every day
Should have realized theres a better way

So now I'm a seeker on the sea of time
I search for answers and wait a sign
I scan the heavens and the stars at night
I brave the darkness in the hope of seeing light
But the reason it is hidden by those who know
By the generals and their armies and wherever they go
Just keeping on searching for it every day
For it's the seeking that makes the reason go away

Hunt and seek and search and try
Walk and climb and soar and fly
Twist and turn and spin and whirl
Rock and roll and dance and sing
Wish and want and hope and ring
Weep and mourn and scream and cry
Learn and laugh and love and change the reason why

Restart

"A tiny boat in an ocean,
an insignificant dot on the landscape,
for an instant in eternity."

Greater London Metropolis, United States of Europe, December 2048.

The year following the end of the ten-year global recession and the month the Middle East Peace conference brought a fragile end to the Israeli/Iranian war Rogier walked the streets of the city looking for excitement. It was even during daylight, a dangerous occupation, but late on a Saturday night some would have called it suicide.

Rogier continued to look over his shoulder keeping an eye on dark doorways and anyone that looked suspicious who came towards him. Every so often his heart leapt a bit at a dark shape or a noise where none should have been. Rogier tapped his inside jacket pocket, the small wadge of money was there and he could feel the weight of it against his breast. Safe. It was safe.

He remembered in his youth walking across Leicester Square with his uncle. In 2010 it had teamed with life but after so many terrorist attacks, two depressions and it being closed for some years few crossed it anymore sticking to the main Shaftsbury Avenue thoroughfare and the one or two theatres which were still open, most dedicated to Andrew Lloyd Webber's back catalogue.

He reached the other side of Leicester Square and was immediately approached by two working girls who smiled at him hoping to turn a trick. After the new virulent strain of AIDS nowadays sex, even protected, with anyone who you did not have a clear history of was worse than Russian roulette. But there were still some who took the risk.

He crossed the street to the a building that in its heydays had presented classic drama - Olivier, Jacobi, McKellen, Sher, Branagh - the greats - but the instant media revolution had put an end to all that.

The theatre - renamed "Reality Check" now served as the only ETV - Entertainment Telepathic Vortex - in London or indeed Northern Europe. There were others of course, one in New York and another in Dubai and those used for scientific and weapons research but they were incredibly expensive to run and utilise. Those open for civilian use like this one charged clients the equivalent of the average month's salary for a 30-minute experience.

Rogier had had the experience recommended to him by his boss who had been given a Reality Check ride as a 10-year long service award by his company. He had chosen to visit the rainforests of the Jurassic age which for the last three months he had not shut up about.

Some chose to meet Jesus or their favourite movie or rock star, other chose more explicit experiences which Rogier could only imagine.

He swiped his identity card into the entry system and placed his hand on the pad and stared at the blue spot for finger print and retina scan. After a second the door clicked and he was asked by an electronic voice to step inside.

The entrance was not unlike that of a theatre, brass fittings, velvet and red plush carpet.

As he looked around and gazed up at the ostentatious candelabra he was greeted by an attractive young lady, smartly dressed in a pin stripe suit and crisp white blouse.

"Mr Van der Pol I presume?" she asked. Rogier nodded and was invited to take a seat on the sofa.

"Now first things first. You have brought the appropriate fee? In cash?" she said.

Rogier dipped into his pocket and handed the woman the envelope, "That will do nicely. I'll check it and give you a receipt of course with you souvenir digi-chip - you'll be able to play back your experience on any top range Mac or high-end Win-mac."

She handed him a cocktail - pre-mixed to his order and opened her pad. "Now. Just give us a few minutes to get you examined and we'll get you started."

She said, "I want to check that the system is programmed exactly for your requested ride. Dr Redstone will be with you momentarily."

She left him seated on the sofa with a non-alcoholic cocktail and he settled back in the chair and picked up one of the old magazines – reproduction versions of "Hello", "Vogue" and "Mojo" were strewn before him. He picked an old copy of "Q" and began reading an interview with David Gilmour. His uncle had raved about Pink Floyd's music but somehow he couldn't get it.

Just as he began to relax, a white-coated young man appeared. "Mr Van der Pol? If you'd like to come with me we'll go through the 'pre-flight' and make sure you're fit and good to go."

He was led into a small surgery room with a reclining leather chair, rather like that of a dentist, and an array of instrumentation.

"Now this won't hurt a bit," the doctor said, "If you just lie down the system will check your various medical and psychological conditions and we should get a read-out within a few minutes."

Rogier lay back and placed his right arm into the rest and placed his hand on the sensors. The doctor placed a strap lightly around his wrist and took a seat at the main console.

The chair began to recline and a scanner appeared from the ceiling and began to move along his body.

The doctor began to check the many and varied readings nodding and occasionally muttering "okay" to himself.

There was a sudden treble beep and the scan returned to its home in the ceiling and the chair began to return to a normal position.

"Excellent state of health Mr Van der Pol. Heart, breathing, eye sight. All normal. Lungs, kidneys and liver working at 90% of efficiency due to normal level of pollutants in the environment. Nothing at all abnormal. You're good to go!"

At that moment the door opened and the smart blonde young lady appeared and smiling said, "Great! Lets get you strapped in!"

He was led up to the next level and taken into a large room which Rogier surmised was the old grand circle of the theatre. In the centre was a large chair but in front of him towards where one would expect to the see the stage, was darkness.

"I have to say your requested ride is fascinating. You must be very excited." Rogier nodded and sat in the chair. It was big, plush and comfortable and seemed to envelope his body and he felt weightless.

"Now let me explain how this works!" the lady said smiling with excitement.

"Once we've got you strapped into the chair, we'll place the vortex helmet over your head and it will take a few seconds to power the ETV to full strength. You will hear a loud single beep followed by the message 'Please begin you ride' and you can begin moving normally, walking, talking, interacting - you will be part of the world. It will be as real as this one. You control your movement by thought - you just need to think what you want to do. "

"Now safety issue! Throughout the ride your right hand will be within a glove and you will be gripping a security joy-stick. If for any reason you do not want to continue your journey simply press the red button on the top of the joystick. The joystick is important - it is the only thing that connects you with this world and the universe you have chosen to visit."

Rogier nodded, "I understand," he said.

The girl placed his hand in the glove and made sure it was connected and secured to the joystick. She strapped his ankles and left arm into the chair and stood in front of him.

"Now. I will return to the control room and as I do so the helmet will lower over you head. You will hear a 30-second countdown at the end of which you should hear the confirmation message. Enjoy your ride!" she said and flicked a switch at the back of the chair. The helmet began to descend over his cranium. Rogier could feel the various sensors make contact with the nodes and medians around his head.

Then the countdown began, "30, 29, 28...."

Rogier took a deep breath. He hoped to God he'd done the right thing.

"25, 24, 23, 22, 21..."

He bit his lip in anticipation. He couldn't see a thing and the countdown seemed to last an eternity.

"15, 14, 13, 12..."

Any second and? Well he really didn't know what to expect.

"7, 6, 5, 4, 3, 2, 1." There was a long beep and flash of white light that blinded him for an instant and "Please begin you ride."

Suddenly he felt himself moving at tremendous speed and for a moment he felt very afraid. He was unsure how to control the machine. Then he remembered and simply thought "Stop!"

Instantly the movement ceased. He looked around himself. He was standing on a platform, it seemed to him it was made of glass. Below him was the earth such that it filled his field of vision below. Ahead and to the left was the sun and he could feel its heat. To the right was the moon and before him was the expanse of space.

He took a deep breath and then thought, "Go!" At once he moved forward such that the earth, sun and moon disappeared behind him. Within a second he'd passed Mars, Jupiter, and Saturn and in another second was outside the solar system.

He moved effortlessly past worlds, planets, galaxies, stars and all of creation.

With the exception of his right arm locked onto the joystick his movement was uninhibited. He could turn around, move around on the platform and he seemed somehow protected by the awesome speed at which he was travelling.

He passed through the centre of galaxies many light millennia across within seconds, all the while moving towards his destination. As far as he could understand he was defying the laws of physics, travelling through time and space at many times the speed of light.

He looked ahead and realised that the swirl of stars and galaxies seemed to cease. In the distance was a tiny white speck which got larger and larger with each second.

He looked around himself and realised he was surrounded by a void. Blackness, darkness, nothingness. For a moment he felt afraid and again stopped his progress. Again the platform on which he was standing came to an abrupt halt.

His heart began to pound and he realised that the emptiness made him feel extremely insignificant. Ahead of him the speck had become a small white disk, glowing and pulsating, and he drew comfort that his destination was before him.

He took a gulp and again the platform began his journey forward. After a few minutes the disk grew larger and larger and Rogier realised it was a small planet, much the same size of earth which pulsated and glowed from white through all the colours of the spectrum to white again.

Rogier began to slow his movement and then brought the platform to a gentle stop.

Yes, this was his destination. He had arrived at the heart of all things, the centre of the universe, the start of creation.

With fascination he watched the world as it grew and glowed, as it waxed and waned, as it changed through every colour that he had ever seen and through many he had not.

Then a voice spoke to him in his head.

"Welcome traveller. Is this what you seek?"

Rogier's mouth was dry but he managed to whisper, "Yes!"

"Does it please you to see the beginning of all songs?"

"Yes!" Rogier was mesmerised.

"You have travelled far. Do you have a question?"

Rogier took a deep breath, "Yes. Yes I do."

"You may ask it," the voice said.

"Are you the creator? Are you God?" Rogier asked.

"I am the creator. But I am not God," the voice said. "God is in men's hearts and is what they choose God to be."

Rogier found the answer enigmatic, "But if you are not God how can you be the creator?"

"I created this space, the beginning of all things, created the explosion of life that started it all. God is an expression of the process. Even I believe in God."

"I don't understand," Rogier said.

"Evidently. All that you see, touch, feel, all life was created by the explosion your scientists call 'The Big Bang'. I created that explosion from which all life in your universe has grown and evolved," the voice said.

"Then you are God!" Rogier said.

"By no means." The voice said, "Simply the creator of life in your universe. Merely a scientist. Look I'll show you."

Suddenly the disk began to shimmer until it seemed to Rogier he was looking into a mirror. The mirror began to clear and he realised that he was looking down on a laboratory. On the side bench were rows and rows of large crystal globes each of which stood on a small wooden pedestal.

Each globe twinkled and glowed and swirled with a thousand thousand stars and galaxies. Next to one a man stood gazing down into a large microscope. He stood up, smiled and waved.

"This is your universe here," and he pointed to the globe next to him.

Rogier realised that his mouth was gaping wide. He looked down at the joystick and the red button on the top of it.

"In fact you have come at a very opportune time," the man said, "We have realised that the experiment on this sphere has reached its conclusion."

"...Conclusion?" Rogier asked.

"Yes, we've realised we've learned all we can learn from your world. The experiment has run its course."

"But what does that mean?" Rogier said his voice suddenly full of fear.

"We are about to restart the experiment in Globe 42. In fact if you wait a few seconds you can begin the process yourself."

Suddenly the disk began to shimmer and then displayed the message: "Please Press Click to Restart."

Rogier looked down at the joystick and the red button on which his thumb rested.

"Just click the button when you're ready..." the voice said.

Lord of Light (Hymn)

Lord Who Made the Shining Sun,
God Who Made the Stars Above
Made Us See Your Guiding Light,
Made Us See Eternal Love
Lord of Grace and Lord of Truth,
Gave Us Hope and Gave Us Peace
Thank You For Our Friends and Kin,
Thank You for Our Joy This Day

And Protect Us from the Hurt,
And Protect Us from the Pain
When the Road is Long and Hard,
When the Thunderstorm is Loud
Make Us Strong and Keep Us Warm,
Make Us Human, Keep Us Proud

Guide Us Through Those Days Ahead,
Guide Us at Our Journey's Start
Keep This Warmth Inside Our Souls,
Keep this Love Deep in Our Hearts

Hold Us in Your Loving Arms,
Hold Us Deep Inside Your Love
Lift Us When We're Cold and Dark,
Lift Us to the Day from Night

Lord Who Made the Shining Sun,
God Who Made those Stars Above
Made Us See Your Guiding Light,
Made Us See Eternal Love
Lord of Grace and Lord of Light,
Gave Us Hope and Gave Us Peace
From the Day You Came Into Our Lives…

Learning to Fly

"In every brave decision, there is courage and a leap of faith.
A place where angels fear to tread."

They are the "Warriors of Light". They are forever with us and forever listening.

Their motto is simple, "Love - Life - Light".

They are eternal warriors fighting the darkness and helping those pass to the light.

And although they are eternally there, we surround ourselves with the white noise of life, IPods and mobiles and radio and traffic and TV and interminable sound which blocks our senses so that we cannot hear their words, feel their warmth or take they guidance.

They forever listen. Listen for the pain of those on earth and to rescue those in need. Then one night they hear a desperate lonely voice in the darkness:

"...this spiralling that drifts like mist through my soul greeting the lost spirits with open arms embracing the pain of a thousand disappointments holding me in its folds of comfort bringing wave upon wave of warmth to my dying and forever lost essence.

Where are you now my soaring spirit, why do you leave me to walk amongst the thieves to steal my happiness and crush my esteem under the feet of darkest energy, which sucks like a vampire my belief in the goodness of the world?

And again I sink deeper into the disguise of life fixing my mask and grimacing behind it, sighing with every breath with grief at my misplaced contentment left somewhere back there in the fields of Elysium.

Only at the last will my inner self be revealed as my mask slips into the dust and I fly to my maker to once again greet the truth and love and peace of the University of the Eternal Ones.

St Michael; I am ready!

Treat me as your true son."

High on a roof, high on the highest of roofs, high over the city stood a young man. Below him the city lights twinkled and the traffic hummed to him.

Life went on. Life goes on.

His long coat blew in the breeze and he took a step towards the edge of the skyscraper.

He closed his eyes and bowed his head. He spread his arms, his body the shape of a crucifix against the dark cobalt-blue sky. He could feel the wind wrapping around his arms and legs winding around him, almost lifting him from the roof. He felt light, he felt safe, and he felt ready.

Tonight he would gain his wings. Tonight he would learn how to fly.

He took a deep breath and closed his eyes again; he took a step forward so his toes were now over the lip of the ledge.

He tilted his head backwards and stared up into the night sky as a tear trickled down his cheek in grief.

This was right, he was ready.

"Good bye…."

And….

Falling, falling, falling. Lights flickering past him. Accelerating faster and faster. In a moment it would be over. Pain. Then no pain. Before him an intense white light. Home.

Then suddenly he was climbing and he closed his eyes. This must be it.

Tentatively he opened his eyes again and looked down. The city hummed below. His feet were firmly on the ground standing on the edge of the roof.

Then a voice behind him spoke, "Are you sure you know what you're doing?"

Who was it? Was he dead? Had he jumped at all? Perhaps he had not? He was confused and he thought for a moment. How could he have company? He had made sure that the door to the rooftop was locked, bolted and barred!

He opened his eyes and turned his head, feet still teetering on the ledge.

There was man, tall, easily more then six feet, with long dark hair wearing a long coat, much like his own, which billowed in the breeze. Behind him the light from the stairwell bathed him in light so that the young man couldn't see his face properly.

The man took a step forward and said, "I asked if you knew what you were doing?"

"Of course! I have done all I should do here. I'm finished," the young man said.

"Indeed. Well, Richard?" and the young man raised his eyebrow, "I think we should perhaps discuss it. Before you fall. Before you are fallen. Just to be sure."

"How do you know my name? How did you get up here?" Richard said.

"Can I suggest you take a step back? Or our conversation may be condensed and extremely concise!" the man said walking to the left and towards a ledge where he sat down, his back to the cityscape.

Richard did so too and sat next to the man who was gazing over the city.

"Absolutely beautiful up here. Good view, "the man said, his head turned towards the cluster of tall buildings of the financial district. "Good spot. Good choice," he added almost condescendingly.

The man turned his head and Richard realised he'd got the most piercing cobalt blue eyes he had seen.

Looking at the man's coat he noticed a badge in the right lapel, like a pilot's insignia with two wings.

Richard pointed to the badge, "Air force?" he asked.

The man smiled, polishing the badge with his sleeve cuff, "Well sort of. I do teach people how to fly."

Richard frowned at the reply, "So how did you get up here?"

"Not really relevant is it? That I'm here is," the man replied.

"And you're here to stop me?" Richard asked.

The man thought for a moment, "Stop? That's up to you. It's all about free will you know."

"So why did you ask if I knew what I was doing?"

"Because I don't think you understood the consequences. All the consequences."

"Man jumps off roof. Man hits ground. Man dies. End of story," Richard replied sarcastically.

"As I thought. And the work you've been doing?"

"What? My job? Systems engineer for a bank? Doesn't exactly inspire does it? Doesn't expand mankind's sphere of understanding does it?"

"No. Your other work."

"What other work? You must have the wrong jumper!" Richard said.

The man nodded, "I don't think so. Richard Trevellyan? Born 2nd February 1968. Died 30th May. "

"Well you got the dates correct. And today is the 30th May," Richard said scratching his head.

The man wrapped the coat around him and the said, "Tell me. How are your dreams?"

Richard stared at him for a moment, "How do you know about my dreams?"

"Let's just say I do. How are they?"

Pretty vivid really. Pretty strange. Same dreams over and over. But different."

"Same but different?"

"Yeah. I'm sure I dream different things but I don't recall them. The dreams I remember are like full widescreen techno-colour movies, THX sound, directed by Ridley Scott, with all the special effects! I play the same character. Some sort of warrior, wielding a sword. Always fighting some battle. Always fighting in darkness. "

"And how do you feel next morning?" the man asked.

"Frankly?" Richard thought for a moment, "Exhausted! Sometimes I ache. Sometimes I don't feel like I've not slept at all," he said.

"And you told your partners? Your girlfriend?" the man asked.

"Ex-girlfriend. Oh yes, and she thought I'd gone gaga. She bailed out with some snotty accountant a month ago," Richard sighed, "Probably why I ended up here."

"Consequences. Cause and effect," the man said, "I'm sorry."

"So what are they about? The dreams?" Richard asked.

"Your other job," the man said.

"I told you I don't have another job," Richard said.

"Soul rescue," the man said.

"Soul what?" Richard replied.

"Soul rescue. You sleep. You begin your real work. Rescuing souls from the world between. Always fighting some battle. Always fighting in darkness."

"Fighting? Between…" Richard prompted.

"Between what you'd call heaven and hell," the man replied.

Richard smirked. "OK. Now this is getting seriously weird. You say that in my dreams I rescue souls from hell."

The man nodded. "Exactly."

Richard chuckled, "OK. So, who are you?"

"My name's Michael. I'm your..." and he searched for the right word. A word Richard would clearly understand, "… boss?"

"No." Richard shook his head. "Sorry. I'm lost!"

"Not lost. Simply looking. Still searching," Michael said.

There was a pregnant silence at which Richard stood up and paced for a few meters. He stood arms folded and turned to Michael.

Michael spoke again, "For the past two years you have been having vivid dreams. The most vivid tend to follow horrific human acts - where there is great loss of life. Do you remember last year when that plane overshot the runway and ploughed into the motorway?"

Richard stopped and looking at Michael said, "Yes?"

"Do you remember last summer when that bomb explored on the train? Do you remember when that ferry capsized in the Channel?"

"Do you remember last month when those soldiers were killed in that helicopter? Do you remember…" Richard stopped him.

"Yes, you know I remember," Richard said and then thinking said, "I remember the faces…"

"It works like this. When there is an act of evil, the devil, the demons, the darkness, whatever you wish to call it, take what they can. We, as warriors of light, fight to protect those who should not be taken. It is an eternal fight against the darkness. Mostly we win," Michael said.

"Darkness? What do you mean by darkness?"

"Corruption, wickedness, murder. The evil that men do."

"But how do I take part? Surely it is just a dream?" Richard asked.

"It is as real as our meeting. Some fight the darkness here on this earth. Others like you fight it between worlds," Michael said.

"And why are you here?" Richard asked again.

"Lets say, at the moment you're working 'part-time'," Michael said smiling.

"And you. My 'boss'. You'd like me to work full-time?" Richard said.

"Well you are very good at what you do!" Michael said.

"Thank you. First praise I've got from a superior."

"Oh, I am not your superior. By no means. I've just been doing the job longer," Michael smiled.

"So why did you stop me jumping?" Richard asked.

"Consequences," Michael said, "If you'd have jumped and you hadn't made a clear choice we may not have saved you."

"And if I don't jump?" Richard asked

"You would still die today. In some other way, again without having made a clear choice," Michael said.

Richard turned and looked at the skyline again. He listened to the hum of the traffic. He thought of his mother and father happily retired in Florida. He thought of his dead-end job.

He thought of his lack of motivation. He thought of the evil that men do and thought that for once he would like to be the change he'd like to see in the world.

"Today is a good day to die," Michael said smiling.

"Okay. Full time," Richard said proudly.

"Good. I knew it," Michael said and he shook Richard's hand warmly. "I told them you would."

"Them?"

"A long story. Later," Michael said.

"And what next?" Richard asked.

"A leap of faith. Time to learn how to fly and you get your wings," Michael said.

Then they walked to the edge.

They looked at each other and smiled. This was going to be good.

High on a roof, high on the highest of roofs, high over the city stood a young man. Below him the city lights twinkled and the traffic hummed to him.

Life went on. Life goes on.

His long coat blew in the breeze and he took a step towards the edge of the skyscraper.

He closed his eyes and bowed his head. He spread his arms, his body the shape of a crucifix against the dark cobalt-blue sky. He could feel the wind wrapping around his arms and legs winding around him almost lifting him. He felt light, he felt safe, and he felt ready.

Tonight he would gain his wings. Tonight he would learn how to fly.

Smiling

I'd walk a hundred thousand miles and wrestle an anaconda
I'd swim the Nile or Amazon (whichever river's longer)
I'd jump the Grandest Canyon on a Honda motorbike
I'd stem an *overstroming* using a finger in a dyke
I'd walk on burning coals or snooze on beds of nails
I'd let you film a DVD to show in case I fail
I'd pick a single red, red rose and take a parenting test
I'd sift through every grain of sand to find the one that's best
I'd sing a Verdi opera or learn to dance the tango
I'd even take my supplements or eat lemon, lime or mango
You see I'd do all of these things (but I'm sure you wouldn't ask)
Every quest I'd do for you and savour every task
Or wait for just a glint of sun that comes before the dawning
To see the love that's in your eyes on each and every morning.

Dawn of Wisdom

"Breathe; breathe in the air of truth and love and hope
Feel the warmth glow inside like a fire that will burn forever"

It is the early Sunday morning stillness; before the sun beats down to heat the lush valley. Echoing around the rocks is the tolling of a single distant bell, calling the faithful to prayer and devotion in the chapel. The chatter of a thousand birds bustling in the bushes on another new day and the solemn bark of a dozing dog waking to the rustle of the trees.

The undulating land below me is a patchwork of meadows and olive groves, the occasional yellow wash of buttercups and lush green of a pasture. The mountains fringing the horizon no longer topped with snow already look baked, distant and desolate.

High on a hill, comfortable in a wicker chair, I sit and watch, as the sun casts the first shadows over fields and farms, and I listen in silence to the wonderful world waking with a silent yawn.

But out there, out there in this land of love and light, something stirs, something dark and insidious which makes the bile rise and an uncontrollable hatred stir. It is something wild, wicked and evil. A darkness that blights our lives and can break the spirit. A wickedness that hides in us all, which we suppress in our happiness and release in our uncaring moments.

It is man's inhumanity to man that is so often seen, so often forgotten, but never forgiven. A burden, which, unchecked, we carry to our graves, fuelling our bitterness and cynicism extinguishing the candle of hope so that we live in the darkness of despair.

Oh, but what a wonderful world where God is all around us, where He begs us to see His works and listen to the sound of the grass growing.

Would it were all that simple!

For we hurtle through the days that blur one on top of another as if it was some ungodly race for survival.

We do not see the love, the light of eternity which is the reason we grow and progress, to be reborn life on life, an ever opening flower that blossoms with colour and beauty.

So, we wish for wisdom and knowledge, the ability to come to terms with life's sorrow.

And we hope for peace and contentment and freedom from empty, soulless pursuits.

Ah, but if we sit for a moment. In peace and tranquillity. If we listen and trust. If we look into ourselves.

In our hearts a tiny ember flickers to ignite a fire so bright not even cruelty can wash it out.

You see, my sons, my daughters, we all possess that light if only we could see it!

Amen.

The Promise

When Your Are Cold, I'll Warm You
When You Are Lost, I'll Find You
If You Are Tired, I'll Hold You
If You Are Down, I'll Lift You
To Support and Shoulder, To Protect and Comfort
To Guide and Light Your Way
To Be Ever There When You Need Me
As Your Rock and Foundation
Not to Own or Possess,
Not to Demand or Expect,
Not to Control or Limit
But to Grow and Share This Great Journey,
As Companion, Partner,
Best Friend, Spouse and Lover
In A Sacred Partnership.
The Unity of Two Souls as One.
With the Eternal Joy in Having Found Each Other
All These Things Are Yours.
Above All These,
I Promise I Will Love You
With All My Heart, With All My Soul, With All My Life
Without End...
We Say These Things So That All May See and Know
Our Love For Each Other

Mark and Ingrid Griffin
Drum Castle, Aberdeenshire

13th May 2000

Final Thoughts

A wise man once noted that no one ever said on their death-bed,
"I wish I had spent more time at work".
I just wish I had listened sooner.

One New Year's Eve, after having particular gloomy thoughts of the coming year, someone once told me, "Ach! Stop your worrying! You have a roof over your head, fire in the hearth, family at your side and food in your belly. You have everything."
He was right.

Don't do it for promotion.
Don't do it for money.
Don't do it for praise.
Do it for yourself.
Do it because its your eyes
you have to look at in the mirror everyday.

By the Same Author

Biography

1994 **Vangelis: The Unknown Man**

Novels

1997 ***going home.***

2006 *Richard of Eastwell*

2007 The Cathar Prophecy

2009 Fairytales, Poems and Prophecies

About the Author

Mark J.T. Griffin

(comes from lots of different places but this time around) was born in March 1958 in Wolverhampton.

He lives in Warwickshire with his wife Ingrid, Sam and Lily the Labradors and cat Bramble.

He divides his spare time between writing, music, drama and theatre. Since the mid-eighties he has written numerous articles and short stories on subjects ranging from clocks to computers to Custer.

In 1994 he wrote the biography, **Vangelis: The Unknown Man** and in 1997 the new age adventure novel ***going home***. This was following in 2006 by the novel *Richard of Eastwell* based on his love of history and theatre. In 2007 his third novel followed, The Cathar Prophecy.

Fairytales, Poems and Prophecies is his first collection of short stories and poetry.